Tales From the River Bottoms

Merle Hanson

WAGONBRIDGE PUBLISHING

2022

Copyright © 2022 Merle Hanson
Cover Photo Copyright © Joan Ella McGill

All rights reserved. No part of this book may be reproduced, stored in a retrieval system, or transmitted in any form or by any means electronic, mechanical, photocopying, recording, or otherwise without the written permission from the author, except in the case of brief quotations included in reviews or critical articles in accordance with the 1976 US Copyright Act and amendments thereto.

First edition, paperback

ISBN: 978-1-953444-11-0

This book is a work of fiction. While care has been taken to provide accurate historical background for the work, the characters, events, and locations presented within are the products of the author's imagination or have been used to create a fictitious story.

Wagonbridge Publishing
661 East Howard St.
Winona, MN 55987

I would first like to thank my editor and publisher, Terri Karsten of Wagonbridge Publishing. Thanks also to my good friends, Joe Hughes and Steven Boland, who helped me navigate Polish History and Culture in the writing of this book; the Winona Newspaper Project and the Winona Republican Herald who documented life in the River Bottoms; finally, Science Girl, Cheryl Utecht, who has brought life to all I do. I can't thank her enough.

"We didn't know what to think. A man who could talk with the dead. Not a chance in Hell. Then I met him. He just wasn't wired right. You know how some people are just off? That was Hanson. Then again, he's the only guy I've met who can talk with us."
Frank Brick, 1955. End Stool, Charlie's Bar.

"Hanson has done some good work. In the world of today with people running around with their heads cut off not knowing where they are going or what they are doing, Hanson gets to know them. Today's living folk got no idea of where they come from. People running around in denial. Don't know who they are, and they deny where they have come from, maybe not even knowing who their people were. Hanson goes walking thru the River Bottoms."
Stanley Langowski, 1928.

"It was refreshing. Days can get kind of long over here in Dodge and Pine Creek. You can only watch corn grow for so long before you get a bit stir crazy. Amelia don't like traveling much anymore but every Sunday morning we head over to the Stockyard Saloon in Dodge, Wisconsin after church, taking the shortcut. Ma, she stays outside the bar gossiping with anybody who's willing to talk. I have a beer with the boys. Always a nice day when Hanson visits the stone yard."
Bob Wicka 1983.

"Don't know why a person would want to live anywhere else. Everything is right close. Nature, wildlife, and characters. There is some great living in these river bottoms."
Hanson 2022.

Table of Contents

Introduction 11

Beginnings 12

East End Winona 20

Across the River: Wisconsin 63

Winona Wanderings 77

Rambles 103

Friends 126

Illnesses Abound 137

Mourning 148

Yesterday and Today 164

Introduction

The dead folks talk in the river bottoms. They talk of life as it was when everybody knew everybody. They come out of the bluffs and river, the marshlands and the towns big and small.

I was young when I first met them. Didn't know what to make of the whispers that came from the shadows. I didn't tell anyone. Some things are best kept secret.

My instinct was to run when those voices started but my dad was a Marine and no son of a Marine was about to run. "Face the demons," I can hear the old man yelling. I just needed time.

Those voices don't talk like living folk. Their talk reflects the life they have lived. We come from good, good people. As I've grown old and the gray light clouds my thinking, I put faces, old dead faces, to the stories and voices I hear.

They tell me not to fear the darkness that awaits. Hear the Tales from the River Bottoms as the dead folks talk about life and the things that matter. Come visit they say, and you'll eventually hear the dead talk.

Beginnings

There are few finer pleasures than a cup of coffee brewed over a morning campfire. It doesn't taste much like the chain stores brand of coffee and a camp site isn't anything like the hustle and bustle of a restaurant. I'll take the sounds of birds over clanking cups any day of the week.

Mostly I like tall trees and the sounds of a rippling creek. They give me space and quiet and make me realize how insignificant I am in the whole scheme of things. Nature and its way of talking is good for the soul.

It took a lifetime of living and learning to get where I'm at. I wasn't much inclined as a young'in to sit amongst the trees and sleep under the beautiful night skies, filled with tiny sparkles of light. We sleep in a tent on a huge comfortable air mattress breathing in the air of camp life.

I hope I never stop learning. I always figured when the learning stops dying begins. And while these bones don't move like they did yesterday my mind keeps seeing the beauty and complexity of this world we live in.

Science Girl has brought me to the outdoors. I was sixty years old before I touched a cow or a horse. Some of my inner workings aren't quite right. I have a terrible fear of heights. My mind fills up with thoughts of blowing winds and my clumsy feet ending up in the bottom of a gully.

Growing up in Winona was in many ways a fairytale. We are a town full of characters and eccentrics. A town that provided entertainment from East to West. A good preparation for living.

I slowly sip my morning coffee. The fire of the wood sticks started talking. They told stories of hungry people and grandmothers and grandfathers long ago. That fire roared tales of the depression and the dust bowl, rail cars and no money.

I pour myself another cup as I feel the breeze and hear the creek. I see the dead faces all around and I raise my cup to the people whose stories wake my soul. Ain't nowhere I'd rather be than sitting around a campfire hearing yesterday as I hear Science Girl rustling about.

##

I didn't want to look, but couldn't help it. The voice was in my ear.

"What are you going to do Hanson? You hear us. Eventually, you'll see us. Quite a secret to keep. Tell the world that living goes beyond the seeing and they'll lock you up, call you crazy, send you to the crazy house where people get lost and buried apart from the people they come from."

I gave in and looked at him, shrugged my shoulders and said, "What's a man to do. Two worlds, living and dead, living side by side in my thinking. Same time, same place. Seeing time from different lights and different ways of seeing. Side by side, living and the dead, all for the seeing, of a mind just starting to think."

"You get to travel time," he said. "Quite an experience awaits you just beyond the seeing. Your thinking changes when the casket closes. Living beyond the living. You get trapped inside your own thinking. Big ego's getting in the way. Civility collapsing all around for all to see."

The Red Bud wove its magic.

I looked at the feller. He was dressed in the uniform of his time. It looked like he was wearing the dress clothes of a WW1 vet though I must admit I'm not up on medals and such. It was a dark night like they always are in the back alleys of Winona. We shared the smoke of our times as we sat on the rickety bench outside that old VFW club reminiscing.

"We hoped you'd see the light. Seeing it is one thing, but getting something to register through that thick skull of yours is no easy task. You ran, we watched, and hoped you would survive the journey that a lost mind brings.

"We whispered, the dead voices whispering in your head, hoping, just hoping you'd figure it out. Such a grand world is the life that lives beyond the seeing. People blind to what they can't see, even when it's all there for the seeing."

I asked him if the war stuck with him through his living days.

He nodded and said, "I tried forgetting the grit and the rubble of the killing game. The dried blood of Bernie's brains that splattered in the fox hole as he fell on the grenade meant for all. That taste of blood and the emptiness of life lost echoes through me," he said. "War, never leaves you. I tried forgetting, but I'd come down here, where men shared the stories of time lost. War tears at a man and his soul even after the shooting stops."

I nodded, thinking about the brothers who didn't make it home and their mothers crying as Baby Bernie was no longer a baby, but a man whose dreams and drives were cut short. The dead soldier misses the things that matter: those quiet moments of weddings, baptisms, funerals that touch men way deep.

We come from a people who like stories, tales, the taller, the better. Our bodies, our souls need the stories of yesterday, the stories of our past, the myths we come from. Stories resting in the souls of the living and dead, and our eyes are closed to the dead who walk amongst us.

That soldier faded and another man slipped in beside me, talking before he even sat down. "You wait Hanson. Ain't nothing like I ever thought. I mean look, dead, gone a hundred years and here I am talking. Dead ain't dead.

"I died in 1902," he said. "52 years old before I stopped my breathing. Too young to serve in the Civil War, though had I been born down south I suppose I could have taken my last breath in the war. Death might have happened on those battle fields where plantation owners thought they were lords over another man and his living. Those prideful, vain politicians of the South sent their youngsters to their early graves, 11, 12, 13, 14 years old, fighting a war they stood no chance of winning. Old men dressed up in fancy clothes wouldn't stop the fighting as pride filled their souls, mamas wept, and those politicians never tasted the blood that comes from the fighting.

"Children died and death didn't seem to matter to those Southern landowners and politicians caught up in their self-importance. Not much different than the red coats as they ruled over their lands."

The Red Bud, the magical red bud was weaving its magic, swirls of life and death circling above and around me as the thunder boomed and the rain poured on top of that old tin roof in the alley behind third.

More voices roaring over the pounding rain, echoing yesterday. I could breathe as I stared at the dark skies and the lightning. It cracked and the thunder boomed.

"They used to give that heaven and hell sermon down there at St. Joe's where Midtown Foods now stands. That church was dark with dingy windows and hell seemed ever close. I heard the rants of Father McGillohuey, echoing thru my thoughts. An old Catholic from a family of old Catholics.

"He'd get a going on that hell thing, yelling and screaming, arms gyrating. His face would turn a carrot red. People swore he thought he was speaking from the top of the Moses Mountain itself. You'd see it in the faces of the parishioners long after the sermon. Hell was waiting. He brought in the coins as the louder he yelled the more the parishioners paid."

I took another hit of the red bud and looked at the fellow talking, skinny, and I'm guessing he grew up poor like so many in Winona eating whatever found its way in front of him. His fingers were stained yellow brown and he said that he had started smoking at the age of seven out back of the Kewpee Cafe which used to be a General Store that sold nails and everything else a man could want. As much as he washed, the yellowed brown stains of nicotine and tar stayed on his fingers till his death he said.

"It shakes you like you've never seen before. Dying changes how you see. It gets dark, like the darkest night when that casket closes. Pure dark, the darkest dark sky you can imagine. You don't see stars, nothing but darkness. Death even sounds different. It jolts you and you realize it was a new game.

"You see, Hanson, once that casket closes everything changes. I walk through the time of my living and the places and times of my best times are no longer seen in anything, but the yellowed newspapers of yesterday. You can't leave Winona, maybe it's the river or the bluffs that make you who you are but when the Indian graves were opened death changed forever as the Indian spirits woke from the slumber of dying. Heaven on earth is this valley tucked between the river and the bluff.

"Everything has changed since my walking days. This town was bustling when we milled the lumber that built the West, when we milled the wheat that fed much of the country and when the railroads filled our town with people and products. Money was everywhere and hard work remains a pillar of Winona living.

"I'm not sure I could live in your loud world, Hanson. When you die, keep the TV's and radios out of our quiet world. Turn off the computers and see life unfold where light moves faster than most can see. Death is life," he said and then he was gone.

He left as he came without my seeing. I took a hit of the Red Bud and felt the quiet of life gone as the pounding rain hit the tin roof, and I felt time in the quiet memories of yesterday.

I go back now and then. Look at the places that got me where I am. Places or times that made a difference in my living. Thank you, I say to a great, great town.

I came alive or broke down, depending on the direction you are looking, out there in the apple trees where light shines different. Life tinkles out there in the valleys and bluffs of St. Yon's like it did in the paintings of Vincent Van Gogh and his olive trees.

The dead don't sound as harsh as they once did. They questioned, the voices, the dead folks did, my very being on the road to a better man. I ran when the voices of the dead started circling my head. Today as that casket grows closer, I give them thanks.

The shadows start dancing inside your thinking. Doubt it creeps into that thinking and the glass walls of our thinking break into broken splinters of glass, shattered dreams. What was I thinking they asked? Those whispers from beyond the seeing.

Hard to put a face on the voices as they tell their story. It fills your bones, those tones shaking the darkness right out of your thinking. You break down as feelings are not what once they were. Let it go, let it go they whisper as I rage against the losing of what I thought.

Just nineteen when those thousand voices started rumbling through me. Nineteen and hearing the dead whispers. Not for the weak soul when the feelings and senses start going. Are they coming, are they coming? Fear beyond the seeing is a long windy road.

I couldn't attach names and faces to those sounds of my disease. I couldn't see the voices that talked beyond my seeing. Thirty years, thirty years before all those tones and voices of listening started working their way through my fingertips. In the streets of Winona town and the campus of St. Mary's.

Part of the Joy Davis Ripley Project on Mental Health. Public Launch late January. Third Street, Downtown Winona.

##

Just a beautiful August day.

It was a long time ago now when things became unraveled, broken. Four decades gone. My mind and heart split, they separated. The thousand cracks of a broken mind let me see things in different light. Life seen through shattered glass. My eyes saw darkness lift and I heard the crumbling of myths.

Whispers here, there, everywhere. Tones of people talking, inflecting different meanings. My senses alive and everything loud and faster. Swirling, swirling thoughts coming from reflections and light flickering all around.

Shadows, the grey light, the seeds of doubt crept into my seeing. Shadow dancers messing with the mind, my thinking as all I thought and knew came tumbling down. Got booted out of college, mostly friendless except for the narratives rolling through my thinking. Took me eleven years to get through the University. It's a disease most suffer alone though it touches many. We ain't always the easiest to get along with as our minds move in 50 different ways.

I had been out drinking. Steves, Nasty Habit, Charlie's, MQ. I was seeing life through a different lens called Schizophrenia. A separation of the mind and body. Old Greek word meaning split mind.

The town seemed darker back then, quieter. Town forefathers weren't interested in spending money on extra light bulbs and so the streets in this town surrounded by bluffs and water are dark.

The old big brick buildings were owned by frugal men who watched every penny. There were cobblestone alleys and back door stoops. A light halfway down the alley. Mostly dark, pitch black. I sat on a back alley stoop, just off Second and Center, near the Latsch building, and had myself a smoke thinking about yesterday gone.

I knew they would show up. I could hear my old man, saying 'charge the hill, face the fear' as I began hearing earlier times. Mud-soaked streets and trains. Wagons and people walking in every direction, a boom town along a river on an island.

Rich men in fancy clothes walking next to the poorest of workers unloading the boats and the trains of supplies and cargo which helped build the west. A mad rush of people. Land they could call their own. A place where man could control his own destiny. America.

I huddled in the doorway of that old building shivering, not knowing what to do or say or feel. Living in 1979 and seeing 1860. I was messed up.

This old guy came over. He looked like a grandpa and he said that I didn't seem right. "You don't know who you are because seeing has changed you." I felt his wisdom as he told me that people were just waiting to talk and to not be afraid.

He raised his finger towards the great moon and cried that the Indian spirits still walk along the paths of their burial grounds. He told me the tales of the Lambertons and Huffs and the scoundrels and the saints who lived in these parts. "I've been here from the beginning," he roared.

He got choked up then and said that Lena Weinberg was his only love besides his mother that he felt in all his days of living. She was a success, an immigrant like all of us once were. "She didn't kill herself," he said. "She and I had coffee that morning of her dying at the old Dew Drop Inn and her heart was happy and free. No sign, nothing and we'd been drinking Wednesday morning coffee together for 30 years. It was a cover up: Lena didn't kill herself."

East End Winona

The East End boys ain't like they used to be. Back in the day they'd a tossed me in the river after giving me a pummeling and I'd have washed up down river. Dead. My jaw was sore and only one of my eyes was still open. I don't remember who hit me or how many it took. Put my back to the wall and gave it all I had. They dropped me off at Gabrych Park. Home plate.

I had begun the day on Eskimo Avenue, a long-gone street that reminds us how far we have come. A bar in every front room with a few renting rooms by the hour. The streets were dirt, sand, potholed and come next spring washed out. It doesn't look anything like it once did. Walking through yesterday's East End. I was talking to Rosie of Rozek's Bar as I started walking the streets while telling yesterday's story. I asked for a drink.

"Pine Creek or Dodge?" she asked in the old way of Polish-American talking.

I stared at her not quite understanding what she was saying. The old Poles had a different accent to their talking. A few folks still can talk like their forebears once did and I miss hearing the old folk who didn't talk like the TV set.

"I don't understand," I said.

"We got two drinks. Potato from Pine Creek and Corn from Dodge. Recipes from the old country. We settled on both sides of the river when we came. Some farmed while others cut and piled lumber. Now I'm a busy lady."

I told her I'd try the Pine Creek. Told her my buddy Harry owned the Pine Creek Bar nowadays and she said she never heard of him.

"A Harris in Pine Creek? Owning a tavern in Pine Creek? Name don't seem Polish to me," she said, as she slammed my drink on the bar. "Never thought I'd get a chance to talk again. Thought I was dead and who comes knocking but Hanson."

I nodded, smiled.

I heard the door open and she began screaming at the man entering the bar. "Schlagovski, out of my bar. You aren't welcome here! You promised your hand in marriage to Suzie Eichman. Knocked her up and now you won't marry her. No place for you here. Be on your way before I call the boys."

"But Rosie. I need a drink. Where's a man to go when Eskimo Avenue closes its doors to a man who has lost everything? I had it all, Rosie. I was a cop who got to rub shoulders with his people. I couldn't take it. I wasn't meant to be a cop. No stomach for the dark side of living. Lost my job, everything, and I started drinking."

"Tell it to Father Pacholski and get out of my bar. Now Hanson, until you cross the river and talk to the dead folk, you are really not much of nothing," she said. "Share a shine with a Bronk, Literski, Galewski or Kulas family member and you'll get a bit of a feel for what it means to be a Pole."

I was having a bowl of Snapper stew at the bar. It was a nice day with a light breeze coming off the river. Logs filled the river on the way to the mill where Polish men cut and stacked lumber coming thru Sam Gordy's slough via Northern Wisconsin forests, and family members who weren't Polish counted the money as those logs helped build all points west of this great river.

"Most places, keep the dark meat for their own but Mr. Rosie uses the best meat in his soup. Uses all the meat in his stew."

The stools were full as the old Poles talked about life. Their eyes carried the loss of yesterday and the homeland they'd left.

"The old country runs through me," Old Man Pehler said. "I can't hardly forget the old folk who helped make me who I am. Hope was hard to find in the Prussian controlled lands who got their share of all we did. Here in this great country we work for ourselves. A buck a day starting out. 11 hour days. We were happy to work hard. To work for a better tomorrow so our children and grandchildren could rise up above their humble beginnings."

He stopped and his eyes went to a different place. "It was the saddest thing I ever did in my life, Hanson. Leaving the home country, kissing for the last time my Babushka, knowing I'd never see her, hug her, eat one of her Pierogi again. I was 12. 1856."

"An early stone in your learning," I said.

He looked at me kind of funny. "You talk funny. Stones in your learning? It's life playing out. You move on and get through it. My heart is hollow. The last words she said to me? 'You must go. Remember me and those you came from. Make us proud. Go to the country where freedom rules and change the world.'"

I nodded and Rosie refilled my glass with Pine Creek. I stared into the clear liquor and thought about what that journey must have been. Leaving home, no chance of going back. Across a mighty ocean. Something to think about.

A young woman sat down right next to me in Rozek's Bar. Looking at her made me smile. Her hair was flying in every which way.

"I took one look at the Son of a Bitch and I spat on his shoes. If he thought I was going to be easy he had another thing coming. I might have been poor with nothing going, fresh off the boat, but he was going to find out quick I was no slave."

"You be careful," Rosie said as she filled my glass. "She is szalone kobiety. Nuts, Cuckoo. She is our niece. We figure it was the boat ride over that made her nuts. Anna and Peter hoped sending her here might give her hope. We paid the fee, arranged the marriage. But acting like she did to Mr. Robokatierhowski? I just don't know. I mean she spat on Henry's shoes when they first met. Who spits on somebody's shoes upon meeting them? Much less the man you were supposed to marry."

I looked at the young lady. I asked her if she had a name.

"Parents gave me the German name of Griselda. Strong woman. Most folks call me Zelda. I was a Daddy's girl. Mostly didn't like men until I met Bop. Bops is a good man. He works at the Mill. We live two houses down. Eskimo Avenue, a world upon itself. I like living next to the river. Spring is rough when we got to move to higher ground but there isn't anything better than walking out your front door, tossing in a line and drinking a beer. Free supper, lunch and breakfast. Never had kids. Just didn't work out. I don't feel any regret about spitting on Henry's shoes. He is fine, but we weren't meant for each other."

"You left Poland?"

"Left my parents. Not my choice. They said there was no future in Poland. Left my Grandparents. Mom wouldn't leave Poland. Grandparents were old and feeble. Dad was a watchmaker who had carved out a nice living.

"I didn't take my eyes off Poland for three days as we left port. Seasick. Couldn't eat. That's when the voices started. Shadows in my head. Dead folk all around me.

"Mr. and Mrs. Rosie sent me to see Doc Heise. I paid him with three freshly caught Walleye caught out my front door. He didn't have any real solutions other than he was a fine, fine listener. They still talk to me; the dead folk do. I just accept them. I sit out along that river some nights. I start me a fire. Lots of scrap lumber and cook my day's catch under the moon of the Mississippi. Then I howl."

I took a sip of that Dodge shine, looked at Mrs. Rosie, and smiled.

The inside of the bar was dripping yellow from the tar and nicotine of the heavy smokers. I went outside the bar for a smoke. I stared at the river and tried to sort through all these funny Kashubian names. I was an Irishmen stuck in the East End and I wasn't sure how I would ever keep those names straight.

A man approached. "I made a mess of my life. Died right there in the Mississippi River. Came up down river. Not much left after the catfish got me. Long ways down the river. It was a cold winter. Mostly under ice I was." The man started talking as he sat down next to me. Bug eyed and skinny. His eyes were shifty as if he were worried about somebody catching him.

I asked him his name as I took a hit of my cigarette.

"Frankie, my name's Frankie. Frankie Kerlin. Not the Fastenal Kierlin! My family roots were from Germany and while those Kierlins stayed out of trouble this Kerlin carried the shadow of trouble with him his entire life. If you see Caroline, my wife, tell her I'm sorry.

"I was a Teamster, but my troubles began long before. You see I liked the drinking. Till my dying day, I'd start my day with a shot of the Dodge Whiskey. We all had hope, us immigrants did. Not much else when we started. Drinking got me. Not proud of it. Caused a lot of pain for all that knew me. Been carrying the guilt all these years.

"The night of my last swim I stopped into Stan Pellowski's bar which was located at Third and High Forest. I ran a tab there and didn't have the money to pay it. That's about the last thing I remember except for Anton Pellowski walking into the bar looking for money. When I said I couldn't pay big Anton got louder and threw me out of his brother's bar. I was drunk and lost, and then I felt something whacking me over the head. Somebody drug me down to the river, through the lumber yard where lumber was neatly stacked 10-15 feet high. That somebody tossed me in the river and the cold water of the Mississippi in March jolted my senses. By that time, I was already under the ice and that's where I took my last breath. Somebody left behind a rubber boot, a big rubber boot, and as you see, I got small feet. A size 8 not a 14.

"I didn't commit suicide like they said. Me being a drunk most folks thought good riddance, and the investigation stopped. Only Derdowski, the owner of the Polish Newspaper and famous poet asked questions. Frank Kerlin, death by suicide. I felt fortunate the Catholic Church let me get buried in the cemetery. Not all churches were like that. Suicide was not looked upon kindly in the church of yesterday. You got any idea who killed me, Hanson?"

I slowly shook my head as I took another hit. I could hear a train a coming. Lumber being shipped all points west. I looked at Frankie and said, "A guy with big feet."

I went into Slage's Saloon. 258 Mankato Avenue. It was in the front end of the house. Just a place where the Polish would gather, rub shoulders and tell stories. August Slage was the owner and most people marveled at the man August had become considering the seed of his father, Frank. I was talking to Mae Stromski in my search for the Kashubian soul.

"I was never prouder in my entire life. The kids of the east end waged their own kind of war on those federal agents. Fought the only way they could. Went back home, tail between their legs, those feds did. We were our own little world down East here. We didn't much like government, figuring between the church and family we could take care of most everything. Freedom. The feds had another thing coming if they thought they were going to stop us from drinking," she said as she lit another smoke. "Not much happened in Winona that the big boys of Windom Park didn't know about. They mostly didn't want anything to do with us except to do the work that their businesses required. Frank Gostomski was H.C. Garvin's chauffeur and Garvin let him know the feds were coming and to tell his people."

Garvin was one of the founders of Bay State Milling. His house still stands on the corner of Broadway and Huff. He bought the Porter Mill out of bankruptcy from a fire and the financial panic of 1893.

Mae stared out over the bar, remembering. "Anyway, those dickheads visited Winona. Brought their wives down in a big bus. The local cops didn't much like the feds. Something goes wrong, and the men in blue get blamed. Something goes right no mention of the men in blue. Cops were local, and they had family all over town, and many of them had stills in their basements."

I looked around the room thru the haze of cigarette smoke. Folks were laughing and carrying on. The couches were pushed up against the wall and couples stood close, hardly moving as old man Stolpa played his accordion quietly in the corner.

Mae wasn't finished with her story. "The kids had been hearing the talk of their parents and grandparents and had been saving fish guts, rotten tomatoes, eggs gone bad for a good week before the feds came to town. It was hot and the air wasn't moving. The kids were prepared, and the older folks had been looking in a different direction.

"The windows on that old bus were wide open, trying to get any air inside it they could. By the time they reached seventh coming from third, fish guts were strewn inside the bus and the windows had been slammed closed to keep the folks inside from getting pelted from rotten tomatoes and eggs. That old bus heated right up with the windows closed. East end boys brought out the knives and slashed the tires as the feds took one on the chin.

"Those kids could be seen scurrying through back yards. Babushkas sitting on porches looked the other way, seeing nothing. Let the kids be kids," Mae said as she downed her drink.

##

I was back in the old times, sitting in the alley behind the Joe Kolter Saloon. In another six months the place would be torn down and a new school named Washington-Kosciusko would replace the block of rickety old buildings. The Polish people took pride in having one of their great generals share the school's name with our first President.

A man came out into the alley still carrying his beer. He saw me and started right in talking, like we were old friends. "Not many of us served in the Civil War. That is except for Antoine Pehler. He was adventurous. Couldn't hardly sit still. That restlessness stuck with him most of his life. Took him a bit longer to find the wisdom that lay in old Polish bones."

"When the war started, 1861 we were just getting our feet wet in this country. Trying to survive. It was a cold winter and wind whistled through the old shacks we were living in. People living on top of each other. Huddled together to stay warm. Praying for spring to get here.

"Every spring when the river rose, the houses of the east end would get crowded as the cousins left their flooded homes, moved in with us until the river receded and they could build again. The Polish spirit has long been attached to the river. It provided us food, a place to relax and think.

"I lived with my Ma and Pa down at the base of Chatfield Street. It was a short walk to the lumber mill for Pa. Every day, I would collect small tree branches that I would put in the stove to help us keep warm. In the early days kindling would be gotten from the lumber mill but soon the mills would charge for that kindling. That paycheck would only go so far."

I took a hit off my cigarette and let myself breathe. I could smell the fried fish coming from the Hot Fish Shop across seventh.

"I helped Ma and Pa anyway I could. When Dad died, I stayed in the same house and nursed Mom to her eventual dying. I suppose, I too will die in that little shack at the base of Chatfield.

"My best friend was Joe Kolter. When I was young, I would be here until closing time and as I grew old, I'd be here when the doors opened. It was a hard day when Joe passed in 29. They said it was his heart, but I think those federal agents murdered him. They busted him one night out there in the west end of town. Three stills on the property Joe was visiting. The feds were waiting, and it's a known fact that they'd try and squeeze the little guy to get him to rat out the big guy. I can say today you rat out Big Anton Pellowski a price would be paid and Joe would never betray one of his Polish Brothers. My buddy, Joe, told them to stick it, and they killed him."

I asked his name, and he shook his head. Long forgotten in the annals of time and comfortable with it. I shook his hand, thanked him, and walked back into the Saloon.

They fixed up Sobieski Park. Put up a new building. It's nice and clean and pretty. Progress I guess but as I walk the blocks surrounding the park, I don't hear and see the laughter of children and old grandmothers watching the neighborhood from their front porch. Hard to make yesterday today when there isn't anybody home.

Back then, the little houses were filled with kids who would wake up and head outside looking for friends, a ball game, anything. We ran through back yards, played kick the can, and rang doorbells, hiding in the bushes to see folks get mad. Anything to get away from where we laid our head to rest. Six kids in a house that was meant for two. Kids being kids.

Ambies was down on the corner. It became the Dawg House, then Schneips and is now the 929 Beer House. Bob Kierlin's grandfather owned the home across the street that doesn't look anything like today. Grandmothers used to tell the kids to stay away from Ambies' bar. It's where dirty men get all full of themselves and forget their family is waiting. Some grandmothers threatened there'd be a paddle waiting, while others threatened two weeks of cleaning the church pews at the Big Red Church that's now a Basilica if you were seen hanging around Ambies' back door.

On Friday nights way back when, they would put up a boxing ring and the local kids all aspired to be the golden glove champ who would try and knock the smithereens out of each other. Sometimes golden glovers from other towns would come and Winona boys would wrap themselves in the cloth of Winona proud.

The East End was alive and beer and stories flowed from the people who played on the greatest playground in all of Winona. And on nights when the lights of Gabrych Park were turned on the East and West End joined together watching the sport of the ages, enjoyed by young and old alike. Baseball and Gabrych Park, like peanut butter and jelly, just meshed with the psyche of a town where the river didn't run straight.

Those small houses had soul. A sense of community, pride ran through that East End. The kids from the little houses grew up, started companies and forgot where they came from. They bought six bedroom houses with five baths, a cleaning lady, and a three car garage. Football replaced baseball as America's sport and the green stands of Gabrych Park came tumbling down.

##

At the Hei-N-Lo, Lucille she was telling me that she'd hit a rough spot. She fell on her buttocks. Right there on the sidewalk, even though it was shoveled. The Hei-N-Lo boys made sure it was always done. Most of them were friends of Tommy.

"That black ice will trip anybody up, and it set me down," she said. "I just don't see like I used too. Reflexes, something of the past. Damn things don't work no more. I was who they built the old ramp for.

"Never had to think much about the mechanics of walking you see. Just did it, but as you age you start looking, seeing different. Age gets you. You might be out on a walk and your vision is out of whack. Your depth perception gone, you can't see once it gets dark and the dusk and grey are scarier because you see shadows of things that ain't, but you fall because you can't put your foot in the place where it should, or a patch of ice is where you don't see.

"They put me in a wheelchair, to keep me from falling on my head. I'm one of those people you know that has to keep moving. Stop moving and the demons take hold. My Grand mom had the same problem. I can't be sitting idle.

"Furniture getting in the way, turning, turning in this wheelchair. It doesn't take long to get depressed when you can't get nowhere or do nothing. Tommy, he don't much do nothing being he is dead and all. All these years I can feel him just beyond the seeing. Never quite get a look but I can sense him. Gotten old, don't see, and the spirits move quick. Dead folks are quicker than the eye, move faster than light itself."

I asked if I could buy her and Tommy a drink. She said she was having Patron this evening. I nodded at Gina and gave her three fingers. I asked Lucille what the occasion was and she said that Tommy had died 30 years ago to the day. She sadly smiled and said she misses the warmth of love and that the tequila never failed them.

I asked her to tell me a story of Tommy and she started talking.

"Tommy never knew his mom and dad. Old Ted and Eva adopted him. Nicest people. Tommy, he liked to run, and Ted and Eva were slower-moving people. An odd couple, the kid and his parents. I really liked them; they treated me like their own. He fished and played ball. Got in fights under the stands of Gabrych Park, settling things like boys used to.

"Couple times a summer down there the Golden Glove boys would box under the lights of Eighth and Steuben before Gabrych became Gabrych in honor of one of the fighting war boys. That East End would come alive when the lights of Gabrych Park lit up. Big green stands, overhead covering. Watching a ball game in the shade on a sunny day was as exciting as it got before the televisions and the million and a half radio stations, we got now took away our thinking. And when they played under the lights, the East End came out."

She took a long drag of her cigarette. Bright red lipstick, her lips down a good 3/8 of an inch on the smoke. She never let the cigarette touch her hand once lit except when a drink needed a place to go. She had these cheeks which made for deep dimples when she inhaled. In and out. In and out. She talked between exhales. "Tommy loved fast. Cars, women, music. He'd cruise down third street driving a Ranchero. He wore the Brylcream and greased it well in the ducktails of his time. He just loved to hear the sound of an engine roar. Fell in love with his motorcycle early on.

"I wore a ponytail and took nothing from no one. Only sister in a house of 5 brothers, you learn to stand up or you get trampled. Our first seeing was down there on third street, The Chef Diner. He came walking in with a couple of buddies. He sat in the stool at the end of counter. I was in the booth. He stared at me for a good twenty minutes as he ate his French fries with ketchup and drank his Dew. He stared at me the entire time and never looked at his plate. I didn't seem to mind which wasn't like me at all. I paid him no attention but something, was different. The dance had begun, and I heard my forebears whispering. "You best play your cards well," they told me.

I lifted my glass looked Lucille in the eye and whispered that Tommy and Lucille had a love forever standing. We clinked our glasses and down the shots went. "I look forward to next Friday," I said walking away.

Next week, I came in, needing a place to sit for a spell. It was Friday-night crowded and there was only one seat left at the bar. It was Bob's seat. Bob was an everyday man and had recently passed. At the Hei-N-Lo, the dead always have a place. He'd worked for the chain company.

I felt myself staring in my glass, old faces, old loves, memories being remembered as the whiskey warmed my heart and memories opened the scars of what was, as I sat where Bob sat. The alleys of living, dark life bringing light to my being.

I started hearing like yesterday. One of the first was an old woman. Her long crinkly nose and piano like fingers filled my brain, scarred my heart during those early days of hearing, feeling, seeing things. Always remembering those voices of the past who helped form the person I've become.

"The devil," that old woman screamed, "Going to have his way with you. You are nothing but putty in his hands." She had this big wart on her nose and long, black hair that flowed past her butt as she poured the fires of hell into my conscious being. Life under a bridge in Spokane, Washington isn't always pleasant.

I took a deep breath as I remembered my scattered feelings. A reminder to the life that has never left me. I steadied myself as I sipped the whiskey.

Gina looked at me and told me to stay warm as I heard the happiness of friends enjoying, the sounds of living echoing off the brick walls of the old bar, whose storied past was not always pretty. Known by the different names of it past. The Hof Brau, Snake Pit, Polly's Place, Bob and Betty's and countless others.

You still hear the old stories if you care to listen but listening is a trait we've often lost on the road of life as we pursue the gold and raise our noses at the real folks who toil in obscurity, never knowing if they'll be remembered beyond the burying. I found meaning in the darkest of places.

It didn't matter much to me whether it was the bottom of a bottle, the end of a joint, a morgue, or a psychiatric unit; I learned things that made life worth living. Most men don't make it back from tipping your toes in the world of crazy. Like the bamboo shoot which grows stronger or the myth of a phoenix rising from the burnt ashes of history, life don't stop for no one.

I see the laughter of Howie and Riff and the smiles of Owatonna Flash and his beautiful wife. I sit remembering what might have been, had the thinking disease not hit me between the eyes. The laughter of good people filled my bones, and I marveled at how fast time flew by in this wonderful, old river town where the dead never leave their haunts. I pounded that whiskey and started walking towards Howie and Riff as schoolmarm Buehler blocked my path.

"Sit down, Hanson." She was a 4th grade teacher at the Lincoln School, now gone. Sarnia and Huff. Pearls and a black dress. White hair and confident. Miss Buehler having a cocktail. "Hanson, I want you to call Stoner Thompson by his rightful first name. Albert Joseph Thompson. His name is Albert Joseph Thompson. Sit up straight," she added.

I sat up straight and told her, "Paul and Henry growing up were the only Thompsons I knew. I only ever knew Stoner as Stoner. He doesn't look like no Albert Joseph. I only got to know him when he came back from that war. He was a bit older. All war is bad it seems. Never knew young Stoner. My gosh by the time I met him he didn't know top from bottom. He had the burning, dancing eyes of a lost man. Nam dancing inside his head."

She took a long sip of the martini she was drinking. Gently stirred, two olives.

"He was one of those guys that you tried not to meet in the alleys or the streets of downtown Winona. He wasn't a ruffian, but you never knew what he was going to say. He would get howling some nights down by the levee. Saw he died while reading the Daily News obituaries."

She nodded her head and said, "I read the obituaries every night before bed. A cup of tea and a biscuit. I liked the evening paper. No time in the morning. Death would ripple through town, everybody knew everybody one way or another. Families all living together, grandparents right close. Dying hit the kids hard. The Republican Herald was a great small-town evening newspaper, but Mr. White was a bit more conservative than me in his believing. It carried news from all parts of the world.

"Reading that evening newspaper kept my mind awake a bit longer especially with winter making it easy to start creeping into bed just after 7 as that sun sets early. Hard on the kids, who need the sun and fresh air. People need to exercise the bones when the weather turns cold."

"Could be but he'll always be Stoner to me Miss Buehler.

I can't call him Albert Joseph. I didn't know Albert Joseph. I knew Stoner."

"When you see him give him my best. He sent me an invitation to his high school graduation. Said the time he spent cleaning my chalkboards after school was the peaceful time he needed. He thanked me for letting him clean the blackboard.

"I used to share an afternoon snack with Albert. He lived in one of the small houses along the tracks. His Mom was meek, mild and obedient. I think Daddy drank too much. Rest his soul. Hope in every kid is what teaching means. We shared peanut butter and vegetables after school when the work was done, trying, just trying to get inside his head."

I noticed Big Dick out of the corner of my eye, saw my glass was empty, and nodded to Gina.

"You'll be seeing the demons," he said.

"No way, no way," I said.

He pointed at his head, "I got where I got by drinking that," pointing at my whiskey glass. "It doesn't take long to get the whiskey disease in your bones and when that happens," he shook his head.

He gave me the whacking off symbol and sat down on the stool at the Hei-N-Lo.

I took a sip of my whiskey and told him, "I like dancing with the demons. Reminds me of old friends who threw curve balls. You still hearing them?" I asked.

"Only when I care to listen," he said. "They get worse the closer you get to the casket."

He absentmindedly reached for his pocket. "Damn government," he said "Taking away my right to smoke."

"Sure, but it is nice not having to wash my clothes after a drink," I said.

"Constitution," he said.

"Like you know lawyering," I said. "What do you miss most from your whiskey drinking days?"

"Driving 120 in the black Cadillac," he said. "Nothing like the night air and the awakening of your senses, driving top down fast. With the whiskey in me nothing scared me. A man with no brain as the whiskey wove its magic. That was me in the whiskey days. Whiskey wrecking my dreams."

I looked at the bottom of my glass, still seeing stories wanting to talk. I looked at Big Jim. "Going faster just got me further behind," I told him. "I'm still standing after a life of running into brick walls."

Jim walked away and another man took his place. He had this silky beard that was almost matted in spots and flew in every direction. His eyes danced happy, and his clothes looked like they came out of a Salvation Army back when they were in old brick buildings with dim lights. He looked like he'd spent too many nights sleeping in apartments without much heat on hard floors. Water hadn't touched that leathery skin in a good month. He nodded to Bobby Rut who was now behind the bar. He asked for a Park Beer.

Bobby laughed, "Park went out of business when Prohibition was made the law. People don't throw nothing away in this town. Somewhere, in this town is a an unopened can of Park. Just not in this bar."

The bearded man shook his head morosely. "Adolph, my middle name is Adolph. 1946. 1946 I was born. All the names in the world, but Adolph? 1946, here in the states. What the hell were my mom and dad thinking?"

"Sorry, my friend. You're stuck with your parents. Whiskey helps me hear the dead talk. I get to the space at the near bottom of that glass and the words I hear are alive and real. A lesser man than you would be dead, Jim. You come from the times when a man could make a living with the strength of his arms."

"Daddy had big fists. I was slow learning with big fists." Adolph showed me his big fists. "We started fighting early on. A man and a child talking the only way we knew. Fists. Words never came easy."

I turned away from Adolph and found a thin man to my side.

"It's not such a bad place this other side," he said. "Who would have thought that Lucky Luscious born on February 13th of 1944 done made it to the promised land? Never thought I'd make it," he said. "I mostly had thoughts. Thoughts not so pleasant. Headed to hell. A hot place that Hell. I was scared and never wanted to show it. The fear, the tension of hell ran thru me. I'd fight not knowing what I was fighting. Something else, something else would start creeping through my belly deep down. The devils cave inside me."

His ears were pointed and filled with the cauliflower. "My Kin folk thought I was the devil himself. I come from old ways," he said.

Warts and all I thought.

"A seed, I carry the seed of the devil. It's a powerful thing, a powerful emotion and as a young man I raged, raged at whatever I saw."

"I never met my Daddy," he told me. "I have the face of my Grandpa. Mama, I love my Mama, but sometimes she would laugh, sometimes she would cry. Sometimes she would stomp and sometimes she would sing. Mama was different every day. Something was wrong with Mama.

"I was born in a State Institution. Faribault. Angry at birth to all that moved, spoke. I couldn't see, filled with hate and anger. Emotions running through me. Over here, where I can now see, I see my grandfather for what he was. It must be purgatory to be still clinging to hate. "I must get going," he said with a smile. "I hear the neigh of a horse, the shuffling of some cards and the sounds of a strike on a bowling alley out here just beyond your hearing."

It gets quiet when the dead say goodbye. I sipped my whiskey and closed my eyes. A woman's voice pulled me out of my reverie.

"You needn't have given the sign of the cross as you left my wake," she said.

I recognized Germaine, an old friend. "Well, I didn't want to upset the folks that were attending the going away party. They'd be calling me a heathen and I don't need that kind of attention. People all sensitive about those kinds of things these days. We used to laugh," I said. "So, tell me about being dead?"

She nodded. "You ain't never seen such darkness. Darker than a nighttime drive across Dakota country. So dark it turns your thinking." She paused as she took a sip of whatever she was drinking.

"That's it?" I said. "It just gets dark and a mere three days after your dying, you show up here next to me?"

"Nothing is that simple, Hanson. Tell me haven't you asked yourself these questions before."

"I ain't never seen your side, and it seems until you reach that other side, we are all just guessing.

Johnny Bell, working the bar, walked over and welcomed Germaine to the other side. Handed her a golden liqueur. Said it helps get your body realigned after the journey. She took that drink down nice and slow, color started flowing out her cheeks and her eyes started dancing.

"Hallelujah," she said. "I didn't think my body could feel worse than it did in my dying days, but I felt pummeled when the absolute darkness started turning into a hazy light. That golden liqueur. The fountain of youth right here at the H and L. I want to laugh with my family. One last farewell before I start the journey. You can ask the next guy what happens after the darkness."

As she was getting ready to leave, she asked me, "Do you have any idea where dead people hang?"

My glass was getting near the bottom when I told her they like old buildings and woodwork. The bottom of whiskey glasses and in a person's fondest moments of yesterday. You don't really leave the places of your memories, those quiet moments. That's what they tell me. They like the smell of warm bread. Damn near drives them crazy. Gets to their insides they say. "

She looked at me and smiled as I thought about just another day at the Hei-N-Lo.

##

A sense of a community is what that H and L means to me. Anytime I went there I found a gathering spot where work and religion are set aside, to be amongst the camaraderie of community. I see Dave and Carol, nod my head, and think what a nice place this is. Owatonna was still smiling, and Gar came strolling through to the cries of 'Gar coming' from all corners. Mulvey sat staring into his drink. Good people seeing life firsthand.

I twirled that glass and images and faces started shimmering in the golden light of an Irish Whiskey. I heard the sounds of a metal door closing and a shattering of glass as the window upon which I viewed the world came crashing. 1977 and 1978 were long years.

Closing my eyes, I went back to that time. I was just finishing a shift at Fiberite, a Winona Company that has been bought and sold from one big corporation to another as the smart people who founded that company moved on to other things. As soon as I clocked out, I started walking. I thought I might even walk by what was their family home on Eighth and then go on down by the lake where they moved as their money grew.

The gritty dust of the dried resin worked its way through the air. Those high boys chopping. Chop, chop they went as the fiberglass got chopped into 3/8 inch fiberglass strands hour after hour, day after day.

That dust from the dried resin found a home in my hair and the pores of my skin. My mouth was dry, and my nose needed blowing. I couldn't wait for the shift to end so I could walk, shower, and breathe again.

Past Little Nashville and Ed's, I walked. Some of my buds headed to the first stool they could find as they tried washing the grit of Fiberite from their clothes and being. I kept walking.

I crossed Fifth at Harriet when I heard a whisper. Winona gets dark when night settles in the valley. Winona people didn't waste money on streetlights, and most houses are dark when the sun goes down.

"We didn't build this town by spending our money on things like well-lit streets." The woman's voice grew stronger. "I'd leave this town in the winter. The cold, the dark, the stillness was something I was not strong enough to bear."

I was just beginning my illness, and I tried ignoring her.

"Don't deny what you got there, Hanson. Us dead people want a piece of you. Talking to the dead? You need to listen to us dead folk. In that world you live in, wisdom has lost its way. Come here, come sit next to me." She patted the stone bench she was sitting on. "Nervous? We don't bite; come on."

When they started talking like that, I didn't know what to do. Tell my psychiatrist and he'd lock me up. Tell my friends and family they'd probably say that padded cell might be the place. It wasn't sin that got me to this point, so I was pretty much flying solo.

"Come on," she said. She had long, thin arms and smoked a

cigarette with an even longer filter. Her hair was in a bit of a bob, her eyes had a twinkle to them, and she wore dangling earrings. Distant kindness seemed to be part of her. I was curious. She oozed money.

"You'll find we are easier to talk with than the living. That time you are living in goes too fast for thinking. A race to death seems to be your goal. We have someone who hears us, and I tell you we got a lot more to say. It doesn't end when the casket closes. It's just the beginning of living for the rest of your time. Things we just didn't realize when we were living in your world.

"You've turned off your mind to history, thinking we were as simple as you make us out to be. Easy answers? A whole world awaits after death you know. You'll be hearing our cries and some nights, some days. It'll feel like a full-time job. Pay is poor, but life isn't about money I now see."

I looked at her as she sat on the bench there outside the big house that was once the Lairds and then the Hortons. The Hortons sold it to the Catholic Church, who kept it until 1976 when it was converted back to residential use.

She went on. "I got called a lot of things in my day. I heard whispers you know. The kids running through the back yard called me Bags. I would sometimes get a little high on my horse and the girls would call me Snooty. My name is Herberta Horton." She extended her long, thin, gloved hands.

I told her that was a funny sounding name for a girl.

She laughed and said her friends called her Hattie, and that was her grandmother's name and her grandmother's before.

"Your body parts don't match your name," I said.

She had long elegant arms, thin, alluring. Hardly, Herberta.

"Then look at my feet. As wide as they are long. I had special shoes made so I could stay balanced. In the night," she said, "Moon or not, all our past celebrates this remarkable town, small house, big house and all in between. My journey through death's door was long. Took forever it seemed and when I came to, I was weak, tired, and worn. But it was renewed life," she said.

She was my first face I met that could talk and see from the other side of living. My mind exploded with her arrival, and I've spent the last forty years with those visions dancing in my head.

I shook my head to clear away the memory. Then I looked at Gina and asked for another drink as the sounds of the Hei-N-Lo brought me comfort.

##

Two sips and I was back in those old days again. A man appeared before me. He raised his sprouting, white eyebrows that glowed as he talked. His mustache caught the spit of that talk as he tapped his cane and said, "Hurry, hurry. Hey, hey, come here young man. Hop to it. Now," he added crankily. "You need to find the bum, Kokomo Joe."

I shook my head. "I just finished a shift at Fiberite, had my ear chewed off by Mrs. Horton and now you are telling me you need me to find somebody at this near midnight hour?"

"My name is Judge CF Buck and 'No' is not an answer. This is your order. My diary I put it on the ledge inside the fireplace of my son's house. 315 W Broadway. Harry Buck and his wife Ida. Old metal box, there you see." He pointed across Broadway as he spoke.

The feller wore the rumpled suit of his times. Dusty black, and blue, blue eyes that sparkled and bugged out of his sockets. White, white hair, long and flowing in every direction. I told him there was no reason to be cranky. I repeated that I just got done with a shift at the Fiberite factory, and the sounds of the high boy machines chopping were still pounding in my head. "Never get to sleep," I told him. "I need to shut off the thinking. And you want me to go to the hobo jungle?"

He opened his jacket and showed me two flasks. "One for sleeping, the other waking," he said. "From the stills of CF Buck. Brewed my own, grew as much as I could, house on Lake Boulevard. We all had farming roots, you see. Whole county was just like that."

"So, about that diary?" I asked.

"Dirt, dirt on em all," he replied. "The story of the founding of this town. All the doings, good, bad, and devious. The boys who got their ways and pulled the strings to make sure that happened. My son, the owner of that fine house used the skeletons of the past as he practiced the law. Had them by the balls he would say. He lived to the 1940's but his last years were lost to the forgetting disease and he told me just after he got here that he'd forgotten the box of those last years of his living."

Suddenly, he sat up straight, pointing. "Look, look do you see that? Out there, that light. See, see?" he said.

"My eyes aren't too good at seeing the dead light, sir," I replied.

"It's her. It's her. She used to stand in front of my son's house, every night for three hours, cold, rain, heat didn't matter as she paced every which way. She said nothing.

"He had sentenced her son to 10 years. Theft. Stillwater. He died a week later. Hung in his cell, just a kid, gone before his time. I heard the whispers as I went about my way. Seeds don't stray, the Churchers sneered. Not easy hearing people whisper.

"Got a restraining order against her he did. She couldn't get any closer than Risling's home, direct across from the Windom House. Windom Park."

I swirled that whiskey glass and wondered about the bum and whatever happened to that diary and thought what a wonderful town this was.

Owatonna was grinning. KD was talking about all the hot spots a person could find himself in. Carol and Dave were looking concerned, and the whiskey glass was still telling stories.

The insides of my thinking where the neurotransmitters flip their switches and send the chemicals and electrical impulses around my body, making us happy or sad, were flashing bright. It was Friday night at the Hei-N-Lo, Seventh and Hamilton and I'd had one too many.

"Ain't no two alike," I was saying. "Some think too fast, and others too slow. Seeing life moving at different speeds at the same time. Schizophrenia talking."

Ridgeway Dick looked at me, and I could see he was trying to figure out the wiring in my thinking. Winona Electricians are thinking folk and knew of electrical wiring.

"Hell of a thing." I told him. "Bright lights flashing from one side of my brain to another.

He slowly drank his beer and asked, "You take pills? I mean, they can control the speed of ideas moving."

"I take a few," I said. "I remember when I first got sick. Haldol, Thorazine and Stelazine. My mind was moving fast and sideways too. Seeing things that weren't there. Shadows, sounds, visions. Those drugs slowed those synapses down, the transistors, and resisters inside my thinking, Dick, and turned them into a knuckle ball. Still love the game."

I turned to listen to the sounds of the Bus Boys playing the music that stilled my soul. They had a way of chilling time, and after that last February we needed to feel the spirit they embody.

The place was full, living and dead folks rubbing shoulders, each talking beyond the living's seeing. The dead just shook their head at us youngsters.

Looking at life from the outside in. The living oblivious to the seeing, beyond the seeing as the sounds of camaraderie echoed off the brick walls, in a place that can melt time itself. Ridgeway wandered off, telling me I should see Doc Heise.

I was drinking Patron and it slowly worked through me. Everything turned quiet and warm. I smiled, letting February go. Further down the Patron wove its magic. Light came creeping into my thinking and I saw Jenny and Chris, Mudcat too. All dancing to the Bus Boys and friends all around.

Twisted Sister Moonpie showed herself, dancing round and through my thinking. Piercing, darting eyes, twinkling brown speckles of life, reaching right through the veneer of my being.

"What hath life wrought from your inner workings," she hissed. "What misfortune has the seeds of life sprouted inside your being that caused your failings. That devil, that devil," she hissed, "fills you, twists you, twisting your thoughts, your feelings and who you are. Money corrupted your soul," she cried.

I laughed and told her I was poor as a church mouse and that running into brick walls isn't usually lucrative. "The devil's plight is more difficult when money don't cloud your thinking," I said.

"You living people aren't nothing more than putty in the devil's hands," she cried. "Has the devil planted his seed in your thinking?"

I stared at my drink as Mushy, Wayne, and Deedrick sang the songs that told the story of Winona. The songs of the river and the bluffs and the people who walk the streets and work the factories.

Twisted Sister Moonpie was dancing, a whirl of colors and scarfs, her moving hands causing my already drunken head to start spinning as the music of The Bus Boys and happy people filled my being. My legs, sometimes wobbly and not working the best, began moving, dancing to the tunes of life. Dance, dance, they said, let go of the bonds keeping you in place.

I stared into my drink, saw Petey Hawaiian and started thinking about younger days when gags seemed harmless, and our hearts beat pure. Unburdened yet by life itself. Sailed into life beyond the age of innocence we did. Little did we know where the winds of life would bring us.

"You were going to straighten out this world like all generations prior," Mr. Cuervo was saying. "Mi amigo, how is that fight going for you? Is the world better or worse?

"You must look at your heart, your life talking, little moments. A stone heart is a man who has turned off meaning. You wait Señor, the heart will beat different as the golden, grey years lurk and weigh down upon you. When a man doesn't feel his heart, life ceases meaning much of anything."

I nodded and heard Mr. Jameson one seat over say, "The booze has found your bones. You won't know who you are in short time. Lose your identity and the bottle says it won the war."

I heard old coaches yell to not give up the fight. I felt my inner Hanson rise as Ridgeway walked by saying, "Better you than me," and Cuervo and Jameson sat smugly flexing their muscle. I looked at the boys, smiled, and ordered another.

An old Indian sat down at the end of the bar. "We were here before you white men trampled our villages and burial sites. Progress, you said, as that life we knew before your coming was overrun by the scourge of the white man. We stood no chance against your bullets and ways.

"Childhood, a way of life gone. My myths, my people relegated to the dustbin of history. You were savages as you ran over our ways. It was a peaceful place before you showed up hurrying everywhere, never finding the peace that can settle in this valley."

I twirled my drink and the stories of yesterday started filling my being. The Bus Boys were playing, and my mind wasn't working. Drunk, plain drunk. Wes Streater, poked me in the ribs and growled in that Streater way of talking that the Bus Boys play some nice stuff. He had an ear and a mind that challenged you.

The old Indian kept talking. Talking about spirits rising and the bastard Henry Huff who opened the graves of his forefathers. "Being six feet under wrapped in Mother Earths womb is warm and comfortable," he said. "Like putting your hands in the dirt after a long winter. Warms your soul down to the bones.

"We rose," he went on. "We rose from the comfort of our burial grounds and our spirits filled the deep cavities of your soul and thinking as time passes through. Open up the graves and life changes for all and there is truth to the saying you can't leave Winona. Our spirits fill the streets and the people of this fine town. We filled your being with the seeds of life lived and our medicine men said it might help our grieving. We waited and waited for our wisdom to reach your understanding.

"Our elders long ago gone, led the way, planting words into your thoughts and doing. Death all around in the big houses. Children dying, money not being able to stop the pain of living. There is no place like being 6 feet under, wrapped in the warmth of mother earth."

I thought about all those nights I'd walked through that Windom Park and talked to those who lived before. I'm still searching for Henry Huff, the bastard of all bastards. He road in a princely carriage surrounded by hired hands. He was the law before there was any in his small town. People grew sick of his devious ways and by 1872 he had left town.

The great Indian spirits filled his being and he died poor, broken and alone. A land agent in a boom town. Henry was a prick, a small man by any measuring, a man with a cruel, cruel heart who told his boys to rob the graves not knowing he was dealing with life everlasting. Ancient warriors now out, they twisted the minds and souls of Huff and his boys who had disturbed their deep sleep.

The Indian wasn't through telling me his story. "Spirits, of long ago talked. Those grave robbers got told of the ancient ways, not knowing where the whispers came from. My grandfathers and those before them were buried here on the land upon which once stood a mound filled with the stories of my ancient past." The wise old man had a storyteller's face, a mind usually somewhere else and while he talked about old times, his sentences were littered with pauses and reflections of life. Deep words, dripping with understanding, wisdom, and honesty. Sometimes his pausing said more than the talking itself as that wisdom oozed out in his quiet talk.

I swirled my drink and I heard Jameson laugh; tonight he had reached my bones. I nodded at Gina and turned to face the wonderful mass of emotions running through the bar. Stories just bouncing off the brick and woodwork as I began downing another.

##

"Bless me Father for I have sinned."

I could hear the words coming out of the confessional booth. It was the day of the dead and one after the other the sins of living were forgiven by the priests of the Catholic faith. Mostly good men, but men none the less.

I heard the long-ago tales echoing off the walls of St Stanislaus Kostka church. People talking, words rattling, circulating for over a 100 years. It started as a small church on the corner and grew to this huge mass of red brick filled with pink marble and the most beautiful, light, stained glass windows. For most of its life the pews were full.

The stories, stories of innocence, were mostly heard in the dark chambers where guilt was let go and conscience grown. For those of us with the disease of hearing and seeing the things out and beyond the seeing and hearing, those stories still echo off tall domed ceilings, ever circulating and never quite escaping the church that the Polish tithed and built. Churches scare me that way. I don't care to hear the sins of a person's living. I got enough baggage rattling around in my thinking and that confessional booth is life lived in the darkest of places.

They were all back for their day of honor. Pawlowskis and Pellowskis, Sadowskis, Modjeskis and Kropidowskis. By the thousands. All attending the Day of the Dead mass.

Blue nose, red nose, big nose, flat nose. Big Hands, strong hands, big heart, gentle heart, small heart. A community celebration of the forefathers who once walked the streets of Winona town. All talking, standing and praying as if they never left.

They held themselves in that relaxed way of old friends. Old man Czarnowski whispered to me that hell was not far from his mind from the time he was a little kid until his dying day. Fear was heard in the church, in the sermons, and it rolled off the tongues of our parents like their parents before. Be good, be good, Johnny, or the fires of hell will catch you, trap you, burn you in the land of eternal damnation.

Betty Prondzinski told me she was baptized, received her holy communion, got confirmed, married and died all in this church like her mother before. "The church was part of my life and towards the end I prayed every day. 13th pew, Zumbro street side, every day. Always worried about the fire of hell," she said.

The priest had his back turned to the parishioners, mumbling Latin that nobody understood. The Blue Heron Consort sung the medieval tunes of the ancient church, and I could feel my insides letting go. Good music can do that.

The priest began spreading the incense and my coughing got worse as it filled my lungs. I tried suppressing that cough and it just got louder, echoing through the church, the sermon, the talking. The eyes of the dead stared at me begging me to hush. I bowed my head and skedaddled remembering to kneel as I left the church. I took a deep breath on the steps down to Fourth Street. I saw Robb Brothers Hardware and Kelli's Corner, Dans Dugout. Prondzinski's Grocery was east a few blocks and Gostomski's Grocery stood across from the grade school. Searching for a cough drop or a nickel piece of candy I decided to give Gostomski's a try.

I sat on the stoop of St. Stan's after walking out of the Mass for the Dead where the stares of the Polish grandmothers had sent me scrambling for an exit.

Slit Eye happened to be waiting for me at the bottom of the steps of the Basilica which saw its dome burn back in the 60's. Lightning from the Gods of the Northern Sky he said as if reading my mind.

"Sit," Slit Eye said. "Let the incense escape your body. Let those threats of hell that you got hovering in your head go. Breathe, look at the sky, hear the sounds, the sounds of the neighborhood all around you." Slit Eye, a Winona guy, would give you the shirt off his back. He might tell you a story or tickle your memory with a story of yesterday. Life with a bottle takes you to some dark places and Slit walked them all.

Slit told me that Paulie Pretzel was in town and that the two of them had gone camping just the other side of the river last week. Dark, dark roads crisscross that river bottom. That other side of the river gets you to seeing things on those roads where the big bucks roam.

I asked him, "How's your old Blazer running?"

"Not sure. I parked it somewhere down here in the East End two nights ago, and I just can't remember where. Jack Daniels will do that," he said. "Called Borkowskis, but they didn't have anything resembling a falling apart Blazer in their lot. So that's what got me here."

I looked at him.

He said, "I saw old man Wroblowski walking in the side door of the church, and I was sure that he had passed away a decade ago. I was leery about walking into that church not being Catholic and all. But you face the fear, walk the dark alleys. Least that's my learning. Fear, fear the devil's prey, his fruit. You have to face it to get on in life," he said.

He took a deep breath and continued. "I walked in, sat down to what seemed to be the stares of a thousand Polish men and women. Least that was what I thought. I probably smelled like day old beer but the music of those Gregorian Chanters brought me to early times. That's when I heard you coughing, and the eyes of disapproval shifted away from me and towards you. I slid out of the pews just before you. Incense makes breathing hard, and I was thinking the Handy Corner might be just the place to clear my mind.

I asked, "How is Paulie Pretzel doing?"

He said, "Not quite sure about that either. I mean he was never quite right from his early days. That Patricia seems to have brought him to a comfortable reality. Only halfway bent. Spirits are all over this valley, not just in the churches. Paul, he dared me to spend a night on Trempeleau Mountain. We slept that night with the great warriors who once roamed these lands and now rested amongst the sounds of the river, the night skies and mother earth.

"We built a small fire and hooked up our sleeping bags between two trees. Paul had brought some Cuervo and put some Microdot in the brownies. He was a bit of chemist with his dad being a science teacher and all.

"There are few things more fulfilling quiet than a setting sun on the Mississippi River. Birds and Ducks hunkering down, and the sounds of the night slowly began circling the Mountain. There's a stillness to the air with the bright stars and a full moon shining. Nothing much prettier and peaceful in the world. I started thinking that there was nothing to that myth of the great Indian spirits that filled this land, when the wood started snapping as the fire hissed, and the wind began whipping.

"Voices started talking. Clear as a bell and I pounded the Cuervo thinking it would fix what I shouldn't be hearing. The tall trees swayed, and you could hear voices chanting the tones and rhythms from days gone by, sounds of people talking, noises just beyond the seeing. Faces in the fire, jumping to the snap of the wood snapping. That's when I met the dead Indian."

Slit and I looked at each other. Like good friends we didn't have to say much. I got up from the stoop of the church, and we started walking towards Louie's Bar which was once called Dan's Dugout and is now the Brickyard.

Soon as we walked in, Slit started talking with an elderly lady, Mrs. Tindorf. Her husband had keeled over a few years prior.

"He was a milk man," she said. "Had himself six wagons and employed eight, not including family. We had friends, went to church, and were getting our head just above water when his heart gave out."

"Leo sure was a fine, fine man," Slit said. "Bought his workers a big turkey every Thanksgiving and a ham for Christmas. You'd see him down here buying them all a beer."

"Mrs. Rozek kept him a tab. He'd come down here on Friday and paid for his workers beer. Let a man take a day off even if it meant he had to do the route himself," she said.

"You have my deepest sympathies. Leo was a fine, decent man," Slit said.

I heard Mrs. Tindorf start sniffling, and my mind began flying every which way. I had little interest in the sounds of grief. Not today, not now. I turned to Louie, still serving drinks and thought it's good to have friends like Slit.

"Louie, get me a Hamm's," I said and started asking him if the trout were biting down near Big Trout Creek in LaMoille.

"Great big ones," he said. "I don't eat them like I used to what with all the chemicals they spray on the farm fields which find their way into the creek and into our stomachs. You wonder why that younger generation has such a short attention span. Sugar and salt, processed foods and raising themselves on the TV. I remember when that TV showed up in the late fifties they were splicing messages into the broadcast. Propaganda coming right out of the television."

I took a long slow draw of my Hamm's. Louie had hair flying in every which direction. His hands and feet would get going every which way, and you could just see his mind twisting and turning.

I asked him, "What are you eating if trout are carrying those chemicals in their flesh?"

"Beer, mostly beer from the time I get up until I say my prayers and close my eyes."

Louie was a bit high strung, and so I changed the subject and asked him about the Twins. He started chuckling. "I haven't had so much fun watching baseball as I did this summer. You know when I was a kid it was the radio. TV was black and white, grainy and undependable. Radio was how I learned the game. I grew up listening to the Braves. 620 out of Milwaukee. Spahn and Sain and pray for rain. Did you know Tommy Aaron and Frank Howard played down there at Gabrych Park before the green stands came a tumbling down?"

I took another sip when I heard Mrs. Tindorf wail. I gave Slit the eye. Baseball is a sport that makes you remember yesterday. It doesn't do it for me but I'm guessing Leo used to hold her hand on Sundays down there at Gabrych Park. Folks got all sorts of attachments to things that are gone.

Mrs. Tindorf said, "We've lost our identity, our sense of community, and the world has descended into hell because of it."

Louie was still talking, "That Nelson Cruz pickup settled that locker room and allowed the kids to start growing into men. Why if that Buxton had stayed healthy and Kepler hadn't worn out, they would've had a better year. They need an ace like Jack Morris who refused to let the Braves beat him. Or Frankie Viola. I loved Mudcat Grant. Dominant stuff, you have to have pitchers.

"I once served Billy Martin you know. He came in stumbling one night, that year he punched Boswell right in the eye. He was the greatest guy until he pounded that third scotch and you started seeing the demons flying out of him. I told him I was closing early the night he was here.

"Honestly, I didn't want to deal with him. A fight waiting to happen. He could manage like few others. I sent him to Sloppy Joes. I was missing my Dolly who took the night off; she just knew how to deal with those drunks who had one too many."

Slit was still talking to Mrs. Tindorf who was complaining about her granddaughter from her second marriage that didn't tell her that she was having a baby. She said, "I learned about the baby birthing from Louie himself. If that ain't a kick in the teeth I don't know what is. Nobody knows anybody anymore."

I looked at Slit and said, "That dead Indian was right. Spirits all over this town. Out and about. Hell or high water, dead folks gather and most of the living don't pay them respect or attention."

Slit smiled and said to me, "I got a fattie in my top pocket."

"Need to regain my sanity," I said.

##

Slit was known for the five paper fattie. I was drooling as we exited Louie's Bar. We weren't ever quite sure where we were headed. Still had to find Slit's car.

That was when Duke rolled up in his shiny 1954 4 door Plymouth Belvedere. In it was a Chrysler Powerflite two speed, black, with a V6 and purring like it was new. It was the first year of production for the Belvedere and had Duke held on to that car it would be worth a pretty penny today. It was spotless and this was twenty some years past being new.

He told us, "There's a pre-concert party at Fuzz Hair's apartment upstairs in the Morgan Block. Pork Belly Productions was putting on the party. New Riders of The Purple Sage was playing at the Mississippi Queen and rumor had it that the Streater Brothers were bringing the band to Fuzz Hair's."

Duke had Panama Red playing on the eight track. We passed that fattie around before we got moving, taking deep breaths and filling the car up with smoke. By the third go around we had started laughing and Scoop slid it into drive. We were cruising down third at 10 mph, wondering if we were going too fast as the fattie worked its magic.

Duke kept looking in that rear view mirror always respecting the tailing capabilities of Winona cops. We slowly drove by Sloppy Joe's and Jimbo started talking about prohibition and the effect on the Loshek family. He said Sloppy Joe's reflected Winona. "Old man Loshek had to spend some time up state, like so many bar owners during Prohibition. The boys from Winona bought a lot of coke and pretzels from the bar on third, to keep the family afloat when booze was illegal. The boys from those Wisconsin Coulees would drop off the goods at the base of St. Charles when it was boathouses. Town has never liked the Feds."

Duke drove through the four-way stop sign at Franklin and Third, claiming he couldn't see out the windows. We stopped at the Club Bar figuring we could walk to the party and the MQ from there.

Slit said, "North Country is fine but the rumor that Jerry Garcia is going to show up to be with his old friends means Fuzz's apartment will be full."

So we parked closer to the action, parking in front of the Latsch building near where the movie theatre now sits. I had noticed an abnormal amount of cars out driving around with fogged up windows and thought Winona was getting its groove on.

I asked the boys if any of them could hear Old Man Latsch yelling at the boys working for him to move faster. Two more different men could not be found than John Latsch Sr. and Jr.

John Jr. donated land to the city. He never married and was mayor once upon a time. He was also an investor in the Brewery which operated out of what was to become the Peerless Chain Building near the waterfront and the railroad tracks. He donated Gabrych Park and Westfield, Lake frontage. The wholesale Grocery business was lucrative in Winona's boomtown years.

The boys said they heard nothing and asked if I was okay. I stumbled in answering that the voices of yesterday voices run through my thinking.

We started walking down Main. My stomach was rumbling as we walked past Clancy's and the smell of fried meat filled the air. My mind began to lose focus as the voices of yesterday started coming from different directions.

We walked up the steps and a white piece of paper was hung on Fuzz's door stating parties were being held at Steve's, The Four Queens, and The Nasty Habit. It was signed Wes and John, Pork Belly Productions, October 14, 1972.

##

I was talking to Pete down at the Polish Embassy, as we called the Athletic Club. Pete was a bit past his prime, a little long in the tooth, finally reaching the magical 70 but he was still holding onto the thoughts of his golden days. His hair was slicked back and he oozed hard work, pride, and smarts. He came from one of the little houses east of Mankato.

"This building, the one you are sitting in, stood for so many things," Pete said. "It stood as a symbol of the Polish way, the Polish soul. This building held our best times, our saddest times. It's where we shared the dark days that living sometimes drops in the lap of people. We were a community, a town within a town and everybody knew everybody.

"I mean I was a friend of Mr. Joe Bambenek. We knew each other from school days. The thing about Joe is his remembering. Some men see the big picture and some see the smallest details but Joe saw both. He wasn't wired right in that way. He ran that chain company and knew every part of its operation, yet he'd walk that mail to the Post Office. He grew up right down the street from the Athletic Club. His Dad worked for the county."

I nodded and sipped on my Hamm's, glancing at the Black and White photos lining the back bar of big time sports legends who once sat in the stools. I asked myself where time had gone as I looked at the shining pictures of yesterday.

Pete wasn't through. "I was born with nothing except my Mama's love and Dads never rest work ethic," he said. "At first it was just one bedroom and we added onto that house as the family grew. When the cousins came for a visit, we'd end up with five kids in a room. And when that sun finally rose we'd be outside and running around in America's greatest playground. The East End of Winona.

"I sold insurance and often this bar was my office. From nothing to something. I think Mama was proud when she passed on in 52.

"That seat you're sitting on was where Leonard Slaggie sat when he came to the club. Just like his father before him. The family stool. This was the place, bowling, beer, and wedding receptions. We'd gather here after the viewing and after the burying, raising a glass in honor of the deceased now gone. The Polish way.

"We bowled and we celebrated life and its important things upstairs on the dance floor where our grandparents and parents danced the polka as we clapped and cheered and laughed. We drank to good times and that Polish soul was found as we remembered our roots and where we came from. The boys around the bar told the stories of the people who were there before them.

I nodded. This building was a marker of Polish life and how far they had come as a people. It is one of the places where you can see yesterday in the walls and in the faded faces of memories growing more distant. I needed a smoke as the stories from yesterday crept into my bones, settling in the deepest parts. The Bus Boys were just starting to tune their guitars and I whispered to Pete that I needed a smoke and some fresh air.

##

The cars drove slower down Mankato Avenue back when cars cruised, and people walked. Yesterday life seemed in order. Work, work, go to church on Sunday, and start again.

Time lingered on Mankato Avenue where the Polish learned about living. People everywhere. Ripinski, Rudinski, Ripkowski, Rutkowski -- all walking the streets, socializing in the bars and working, working to get ahead. Down here time moved at a different pace.

It was the place back in the day. Three bars sitting right close, and men have always stepped outside for a smoke and on this beautiful fall night I headed to the bar covered by black top.

The Square Deal was a bar of workers who carried the pride of being Polish on their sleeve and in their talk. Like all the Polish I've ever met, family was what mattered and though many of the boys might have preferred a day on the river providing food for their family, they all made it to St. Stan's on Sunday.

It was crowded, people rubbing shoulders, talking about baseball, family, fishing, and bowling. The Polish flag hung on the wall and an old picture of Julie Wera hung on that wall of the old bar with the Babe and Gehrig. Julie Wera was from the little houses and played on the Yankees back just before hard times hit this country. The old poles were treated with reverence in the bar that has been run over by time.

One of those old-timers sat beside me. "I figure, Hanson, when I finally get around to dying, it's going to look like this. A bar and happy people. We drink the beer, you know, and the Polish heart sings, it dances and laughs. Heaven, it's got to have a river. Without water we can't hardly breathe. The Polish soul needs fish to survive, water runs through us. Name is Rat, by the way."

I asked him, "How'd you get the name Rat?"

"My last name is Ratijusewski. Try spelling that when you are a second grader. Whose going to yell Ratijusewski? They started yelling Rat. Everybody called me Rat. Of course, there was Big Rat, Little Rat and then there was my Uncle Rat. He was the coolest.

"We had fine teachers I tell you. Just getting kids to spell their last names when just a kid wasn't easy. Ain't something easy like Hanson. So Rat's my name."

Another old timer chimed in. "Us Polish got to have beer," Dickie said. "Heaven, without beer can't be heaven." Dickie spoke in the old Polish English we don't hear no more. He spoke it like his Daddy and Grandfather before him.

Maria had poured me a Schmidt. I took a deep breath taking in the sights of happy people. Family related by the Polish heart. Warm, genuine and caring.

So many memories buried under the blacktop or neglected to the point of demolition as money became all that mattered. I heard Perry Como playing on the jukebox and saw the hearts of East End gals grow melancholy.

Back at the bar, I was sitting down near the end of the bar. Lucille and Tommy were carrying on like love birds do right next to me. I was talking with Yellow Fingers. He was talking about the world as he knew it. He was ten years older and knew most everything. Like me, his voices started talking just after his eighteenth. Sunday morning at the Hei-N-Lo.

He was called Yellow Fingers because he smoked 3 packs of Camels a day, unfiltered and right down to the stub. Thirty years later the heavy smoking had left his fingers golden stained and brown. People smoked at the bar, filling their lungs with the tar and nicotine, taking years off not only their life but that of the people sitting next to them. Damn government improved our lot when they brought the smoking outside.

I nodded. Fingers was like an older brother. Seeing things others didn't. He didn't finish his schooling, succumbing to the sounds and whispers of time talking. Nobody could tell a story like Fingers.

Being it was Sunday, Yellow Fingers carried the myth of heading to Church as being proper for Sunday morning. Catholics doing their obligations back when time moved slower.

He told me, "It was damn scary when I started seeing and hearing dead folk. My drinking, smoking, and drug use was a way of coping. Carrying on a conversation wasn't always easy. As far as I could see it was Henry Huff who released the spirits. Woke the dead Indian, lifting their spirits up from the warmth of mother earth. Opened the graves, ground the bones, and forever altered life in this beautiful valley.

"Huff wasn't alone but I'm not sure there was a man more disliked than Henry Huff," he said. "I was just a kid and I'd go down to Charlie's on Main with my dad. Sunday morning mass to my way of thinking. Jesus would be drinking on Sunday morning if he were living today."

"Charlie Beck himself said, If Henry Huff hadn't left this town, he'd a been dumped in the bottom of the river and left for the catfish. Served him right. Winona boys didn't much like the way he locked Mrs. Huff up in that tower. Quiet, quiet town and back in the day, the sounds of her whaling from the lookout tower was there for the listening.

"Huff knew something was amiss. I mean he hightailed out of the town as soon as he could. 1872. The Indian spirits followed Henry and his life. Two of his children died young and Henry sold out to banking and railroad interests. The Lambertons. He lost everything in the Great Chicago Fire and died penniless. His casket showed up on the Masonic doorstep upon his dying for burial. Spirits of the dead they get right inside you. They take over a person and his thinking. I had to accept them," he said. "I just couldn't live in denial like so many."

I nodded and asked Sarah for two more as I took in the spirit of a beautiful Sunday morning at the Hei-N-Lo with Yellow Fingers.

Warron Zevon was coming out of the jukebox. Yellow Fingers was talking about people and time. Old friends who've drifted apart and hearts that have gone cold as life leaves its mark. "I had dreams," he said, "Like everybody else. A splintered mind changed those dreams. Picking up the pieces of what was. I was holding a Deuce in a world where Aces ruled. Life falls in different ways."

I looked at Lucille. She was wearing a purple hat today, with a feather sticking out the side. She wore the white sunglasses, her lipstick, bright red, was smudged, and she smoked cigarettes one after another.

"It wasn't always this way," Yellow Fingers said as he looked at me. "I was there the day when Lucille and Tommy got hitched. August 23, 1969. And I was here the day Tommy died July 14, 1978. It was love, every which way you looked.

"I saw that beautiful messed up woman you are staring at when she was her happiest and both she and I were waiting at the bar for Tommy, sipping our beers when a couple of officers and the parents of Lucille came through the front door on the dark day. She turned white as they approached her. They tried coaxing her to come outside and talk but Lucille stood strong against the winds of pain which flooded the bar and told them to say what needed saying. The men in blue shone bright that day as they told Lucille in the quietest of ways that Tommy had died coming down the hill from Stockton riding his motorcycle, the wind blowing in his face and with a smile on that face as he was doing what he most enjoyed.

"I put my arm around Lucille and felt her insides twisting, changing, collapsing. I felt those building blocks we carry inside crumble as her emotions broke down right in front of me. I wanted to run, run as fast and drive as fast as I could from the pain that was creeping into my being. Soon Lucille was surrounded by old friends and caring people. I scooted out back to the patio, which was once a back yard, taking a deep breath as I left.

"Tommy and I had known each other forever. I grew up on eighth and he lived on 9th. Back yard neighbors who spent summers running through back yards and alleys, ringing doorbells and being young. We'd steal cigarettes from our parents, light up, and spend our days as brothers. Tommy was a part of my soul, and his dying ran through me."

I closed my eyes, tried relaxing, wondering what lay beyond the bend as time wielded its ugly sword.

"Hey Bob, how you doing?" I raised my glass to the man sitting next to me.

He just nodded his head, mind trapped in the world of chain making. I asked him once why he stopped at the Hei-N-Lo every day.

"I work eight to ten hours a day," he said. "It consumes me. Engineering, people, bosses, making things faster, more efficient, and it gets inside you. I need these two beers to dampen the sounds of work so when I get home, I can be a family man."

Bob never said much normally. Mostly quiet. I guess I bring out the rants in people. I don't mind.

"I was lucky, I guess. Death it happened rather suddenly, quietly," he said. "It wasn't one of those prolonged deaths where I was hooked up to tubes and oxygen. I wish I could have said goodbye in my time and told people how much they meant to me. Trust me I wasn't thinking about chain making as I stepped on over."

I looked to my left and saw General Wayne drinking his Mountain Dew. He looked as if he had just stepped off a battlefield and was still carrying the wounds of a battle fought long ago long before airplanes and computers. He had this long, unkempt beard. Scruffy and he had himself a disposition that spoke hell on earth. He was dressed in the old grays of a vet, minus the uniform.

Wayne spoke quietly. "I had stage 5 cancer. I had a couple bags attached to me, but now that I stopped drinking beer it is now only a Stage 4 and I have only one bag attached."

"I knew a guy, Wayne, who should have been dead 50 years ago and that his disposition had improved immensely since he put down the flavored beer water and started drinking better beer," I said.

"I'm not going on a machine," he said. "If I was meant to finally die, I wanted to do it with the wind in my face, one last battle, one last war, myself against the world."

He took a sip of his Mountain Dew.

"Wouldn't want you any other way, General. Pissing in the wind with your last breath." I told him that I don't think that whatever awaits us is quite ready for an ornery cuss like him. Houston, Minnesota boys just aren't wired quite the same as most. Must be the Root River that gets into your thinking.

Bob whispered, "The chemicals rolling down upon the valley that Houston, Minnesota sits in has probably scrambled more than a few brains. Those residues filter into the crops and the soil you know. It'll reach the water table, find its place. Limestone rock isn't that hard." He kept carrying on about the boys from Houston, Minnesota. "That corn that gets chewed and works its way into the muscles and bones of the beef cattle who eat it. Sugars, sugar in everything. No wonder why we got ourselves so many large belly's sitting on bar stools."

"I know, I know," General Wayne said. "Engineer thinking. Got to get it out of me before I get home. Two beers, two beers is all," he nodded saying, "That comes from having a job which demands straight line, bottom line thinking. That's why I stopped when living. Get it out of me, let my mind relax. Didn't have to say nothing, just let things go. The mouth follows the mind you know. Us engineers got a straight-line way of thinking to us."

I nodded and asked Gina for another.

"I grew up in this neighborhood. 611 E Wabasha. I've been wanting to meet you, Hanson. Life wasn't easy. Me or my brothers. Dad drank. He wasn't a nice man. We fought. He used to beat me. I grew up. I turned 17 and I popped him. I'd a killed him if I hadn't joined the service.

"I liked running around, smoking cigarettes and looking tough. I knew everything. I loved dames and didn't like school. Factory worker. Most thought I'd end up working at the Swift Plant down there in the east end.

"I joined the Army. Everyone was proud. I remember grandma lovingly tapping my shoulder and saying I'd be a fine, fine soldier. I liked the military life. Basic training, the first taste of wars. Blood, killing, that grit sticks inside you.

"We walked right into an ambush. Hells beginning. Long marches in winter, wind blowing. 20, 30 below. Just a thin jacket. They gave us no food and water, just crumbs and bad shoes, sleep two hours, get up and march. That loudspeaker blaring the tales of all that is wrong because of us. Months on end till time lost meaning.

"We would march through a town, and they would pelt us with rocks. We had no idea what the people of Korea were saying, what they believed, had been told to believe. You start breaking down, Hanson and you start hearing things and you are not sure what is real. Louder and louder that speaker talked, no place to escape. Even as we slept the speaker played on. Deep inside Korea we marched.

"Some of us didn't make it back. Died on the march through Korea. We kept marching, no grieving, as fellow soldiers died along the side of the road, not knowing if they were buried or left to wild dogs. That loudspeaker kept squawking how we were responsible for the death, the war, our condition. Turn toward the star of communism they said. And if you wavered, they gave you better food. Communists playing an ugly game with a man and his mind.

"It was a couple years before I came home. Lubinski returns home the newspaper screamed. Service clubs honored me paying me respect. I struggled talking, the demons inside tying my tongue. I could see it in the eyes of old friends that Jack wasn't the same. Carefree Jack was gone.

"I finished my life alone. Dying in the streets of Winona, living in my childhood home. I walked everyday 5-10 miles trying to shake the demons of that Korean war. A walking casualty. A shell of a man. My only pleasure was the pack of camels I carried in my pocket."

##

"I'd be going nuts, demanding something to be done about the mess on Mankato Avenue. I used to own the Hot Fish Shop, since tore down and taking a left onto Mankato from where the Dairy Queen stands is near impossible or suicidal with the way people are driving." He looked at me from his barstool. He always sat in the fifth seat. He liked bowling and was good at it so people used to see him done here at the Athletic Club when he wasn't at his restaurant.

"How do I sell this to the factory owners?" he asked.

I looked at him. "Starting and stopping. Starting and stopping. These trucks are built for the highways. Only one way into the east end for truckers and those east end boys got a big appetite with their big trucks and heavy loads. Bad enough we got that one immovable object slowing down the workflow in the train tracks but if you are like me, I hit every red light on the way. How many are there? Three? Four stop signs? Start, stop. All blocking the workflow. Downtime and you haven't gone a couple miles. Now it's your old neighborhood you should worry about," I said. "That's where your myth comes from. The place of your roots, getting run over by tomorrow. Who is going to remember?" I asked. "Then tell those Y boys you just got to drive around a small circle and soon they'll be back downtown."

"This was my grandfather's seat," he said. "Weddings, funerals, bowling, everyday living. We lived in these four walls of the Athletic Club," he said. "Do you hear them? Yesterday, bouncing off these walls. It is right there in front of you."

##

I went walking into Linahan's. I was surprised to see the place full. I had always figured they headed out to the country club after finishing up their day.

Stink was bartending, though his name tag said Jerome. He had himself on a nice black bow tie, and I noticed he delivered every drink with a Sir or a Doc.

A lot of the boys were drinking Martinis. Stink, he always made sure he put an extra olive in the drink. He called it his three-olive martini, and it was his Tuesday happy hour special.

The guy next to me said, "Winona boys have always liked their pickles and olives. All over town there were barrels of pickles. A penny a pickle or a nickel a pickle. Part of our roots."

This was the second Martini I had seen Stink pour him. I wasn't going to stop his talking.

"What happens you see is that the salt constricts, tightens the blood vessels," he said. "Those vessels lose their elasticity; your veins get stressed. Your heart has to work harder to get that blood to your deeper body parts. The smart thing would be to watch the foods you eat, keep the vessels from tightening up too much to begin with. But we got a salt craving. Satisfying that craving gives us a bit of high, an adrenaline shot. Pretty soon you start getting the plaque buildup. Now Hanson, I come here to forget work and now you got me thinking about patients."

Stink had a big smile on his face knowing Doc had found an open ear. Doc was rolling one of the olives in his mouth. Savoring the saltiness of the olive after the cleansing of an extra dry Martini.

I wondered where his mind was as he surrendered himself to the mighty olive. "What are you thinking Doc?"

"It's not the thinking," he said, "but the feeling, the letting go that a Martini brings me. I think all day and when I get done working, I like to turn it off. Take off my Dr. Hat and put on my grandpa face. I feel a release," he said. "A liberation from work and the thoughts of the day. You must shake it out of your bones and this olive lets me release, lets me relax, let go. Makes me a family man.

"Wakes me up. Only two, only two until I can get to the Club and by the time, I've left the Country Club I can be a family man. Even ride the golf cart home if I have too. "Great town, great town but if I tried taking a left out of the Severson Oil parking lot today with the way you young folks drive I sure as hell would have gotten in an accident.

"I just don't see as clearly anymore; my depth speed perception is all out of whack. Oh, I pass the eye tests but moving my head back and forth sometimes makes me forget. I imagine I would have little interest in taking a left onto Mankato today. Never get to meet all the people I did drinking here at this bar. Accident waiting to happen even with my big black caddy. Straight out to the Country Club. Roundabouts make things simpler once you figure out where you are going. Just hard getting used to."

I ordered another and I heard the voices of old shop teachers yelling measure twice before cutting. That's when the guy next to me, drinking something Stink called A Grouchy Bastard, started talking.

##

You never knew what Shive was going to say. He would show up at the Mankato Bar on what the old timers call Old Stone Road in the early afternoon and by supper time his legs and mouth were going in different directions. You used to see him fishing along Shive Road and thus the nickname.

"There was nothing better than fishing as the sun went down. Bats and bugs flying all over, and the bullheads were biting. Tomorrow's lunch and supper, breakfast too," he said. "Some folks don't like the evil bats as they go about pollinating the flowers and plants that feed us. And they eat the bugs which in the summer months multiply and multiply, millions upon millions. They start getting to you and it is swat, swat, swat. Oh, those skeeters can drive men itchy, crazy, nuts."

Doris at the Bar whispered to me, "Those fish he caught and ate down there by the Water Treatment plant had somehow poisoned his thinking. His Daddy had the same problems. They lived in a little bitty shack between the tracks and the creek. Some of the brothers got it bad he'd be saying. They start swatting at bugs that aren't there. They insist they feel them on their skin. We need those bats; we need those bats, just to keep the bugs away."

I sipped on my beer. The Kato was one of those bars filled with good people. A welcoming place, with its Christmas tree lights hanging over the bar helping to keep gals and boys awake. The gals were singing Country Roads and the boys were all remembering that all their parts once worked.

Sometimes I get to reflecting. Old Shive he has been dead and gone now twenty years and his last six months were spent in the Sauer Home. I visited him and he said he wanted to die fishing. Throw me to the catfish he would chortle.

Towards the end his mind started going and he'd say that bats were a gift. He said, "At night when you sleep they plant the devil's seeds. They get right in your thinking. Doubt starts creeping into your soul and I hear the God voice laughing. Make the boys think, the God voice says. I gave you a brain. Use it. Blind obedience gets you nowhere. Throw me to the catfish, Hanson."

Life as a schizophrenic isn't always easy.

Across the River: Wisconsin

"Welcome to Dodge," the old timer said as we sat near the back wall eating a lunch prepared by a man wearing an earring in his nose.

The bar inside doesn't match the outside siding covering yesterday. I was expecting broken bar stools and rickety tables. Dusty glasses and a back bar with half empty brandy bottles that had been there forever. Boys with their heads glued to the bar, hardly breathing, much less talking. It didn't take long before I heard yesterday's voices.

"Joe, Joe Slaby," he said. "Took my last breath here in Dodge. Been here ever since. Watching time fly. Mostly forgotten now, but I was once the talk of the town. I drank every day. Here and at the Longbranch Saloon, Slage's Hotel. A short walk from my home."

I took a sip of my Hamm's and popped a batter fried mushroom in my mouth. Tasty and the batter complimented the mushroom. The dude with a ring in his nose can cook.

"I was a tailor," Joe went on. "I stitched and mended. I liked the quiet of my occupation. No kids, no wife in my life. I was an only child and the end of the line. The last tailor in Dodge. It had been the family trade for generations. Long before stepping foot in Dodge,

Wisconsin. "

Trempeleau girl, the bartender, came over asking if we wanted another drink. Steve, sitting next to me, ordered another beer and Trempeleau girl brought one over. She never heard the dead folk wanting theirs. A good waitress is hard to come by. Finding one that hears dead folk talking don't happen often.

"I was a perfectionist," Joe said. "Everything just right. I'd get to stitching those Polish dance shirts. Small, intricate needle work. Totally into my work. I wanted silence. I wore a magnifying glass around my head as I grew old. Eyes start working not so well. I'd concentrate harder. That's when the headaches started. Alcohol took my headaches away, so I drank more.

"I wasn't a big man and I spent my entire life being bullied. Alcohol gave me courage but inevitably it got me booted out of one bar after another."

I looked at Joe and Steve. Steve was eating some Friday Fish that looked just perfect. Joe was inhaling something called a grilled cheese bacon cheeseburger. He said it was delicious while I felt the spirits all around me. They fill my stomach and my senses as I get to know them.

Joe went on. "Lonely life and the demons didn't seem to slow down. Any little noise when I was working would send me into a rage," he said. "I had a horrible temper when living. Uptight. I tried holding onto the demons raging inside me, but they would fly right out. That second whiskey and I was ready to take on the town. I sneered in every direction. Once they started leaving there was no holding back. They got worse as the whiskey took hold. I got tossed out of the bar more times than you can shake a stick at. That Pellowski shine ran through me.

"Bullies all around me. I was a small man doing the work of a lady they would snarl. I started calling them every name in the book and they'd laugh just making me madder. They enjoyed getting me going. It was the way of the times, Hanson.

"Kids early on figured they could get my goat. They would throw little pebbles on my tin roof. Drove me crazy. Don't get me wrong, I loved the sound of rain drops falling on that tin roof, but stones were different. Rain was one of the few things that could calm me, but rocks don't sound nothing like rain." He smiled. "I screamed at those damn kids. The more I screamed the more rocks they threw. They grew bold as they saw I was a weakling. I started walking outside with my shotgun as they scampered away. No matter, they wouldn't leave me alone. I never meant no harm.

"I talked to Sheriff Brom, and he said they were just kids being kids. Said he would talk to them. Finally, one day I just got fed up. Took out my shotgun and walked out onto the porch.
I hollered and they turned. I placed the shotgun in my mouth. They stared as I pulled the trigger. I felt myself leaving as the sounds of the shotgun filled the air."

He shook his head and went on. "I still miss the sound of that train coming through town. Stopping, dropping people off. Families greeting each other. The demons left me when I stepped on over. They buried me outside the cemetery lines. Taking one's life was frowned upon in the church of the times. Father Gara was a good man and shortly after they added more land."

I finished the last of my beer, nodded at the boys sitting round the bar and wondered what other stories lay in the deep thoughts of old Dodge.

##

"It's over. I'm done with you. Done, gone, no more!" Her Benson and Hedges cigarette was jumping up and down as her hands moved this way and that. We were driving the short cut between Pine Creek and Dodge. Lulu was jabbing at the air as she said, "All you do is smoke that pot. Never get nothing done!"

She was right. I had a bit of a problem. We were in the truck coming over the hill from Pine Creek to Dodge. The short cut. I was a bit worried. She was driving too fast; her blue eyes were ablaze. I'd been drinking hard for a year. No job, no hope, no future is what I had going. She said she had enough and dropped me off in front of the Stockyard Saloon. I got out not bothering to argue. LuLu was quite the gal and never lost her side of an argument.

Whiskey and weed had been keeping me upright for the last year. It wasn't easy being a drunken Irishman in the lands of mostly

Polish persuasion. I sat, collecting myself in front of the old general store, and smoking the weed grown on the back 40 of Padolinski's farm. I always figured it would take a dead body to get the feds out to the middle of that cornfield if they wanted to bust me. The boys got a long history of bootlegging in the hills surrounding Dodge and Pine Creek.

Padolinski was an old man when I worked for him. Died a few years back. Old Poles grow wise when the graveyard starts calling, and old Pad was no exception. He still liked the planting and harvesting. Told me more than once that was how he hoped to die. The last harvest. But he couldn't understand how come the middle of his cornfield had a big brown spot every fall. I felt satisfaction in getting the land ready for next year planting.

I looked up and down the street. Wasn't much happening. The train had stopped running. The Post Office was closed and the houses all looked like they needed paint. The implement store said yesterday. I took another hit, and I felt myself thinking as I walked into the Stockyard.

I sat down next to Patches. He came from the family whose land helped make the town. Patches and his family owned the Tavern, the Bank and the Implement Company. Not much happened in town without the Hoesley family knowing about it.

Patches was a quiet soft-spoken fellow. Understanding. He didn't say anything as I sat down. Yvonne gave me a dirty look as I ordered my Hamm's. I took a long deep breath and felt the beer relax me.

"We all love Lulu. She is one of us. We don't forget in Dodge. Not much hope for an Irishman," Yvonne said, walking away.

I felt the disgust of the people sitting at the bar. Good people and families disappointed in Lulu and me not working it out. Going to be a long haul to regain any little respect I might have had. I took another sip. Word traveled fast in old Dodge.

"You walked away from a nice farm. Jacob and Mary had only one child, Lulu. One of the nicest families in the area. Would have been yours. Jacob and Mary are feeling sad this morning. Family has been in these parts since the beginning. They always wanted more children." Patches was talking wisdom.

I felt my head spinning. That smoke was kicking in. The light and the sounds were coming from all directions.

"We haven't said anything about your business operation, Hanson," Patches continued. "Family you know. Why right across the bar sits a Pellowski. A great nephew of Jacob Pellowski whose son ran the large still operation that supplied Chicago with much of its liquor during prohibition. Died when lightning struck him. Railroad line ran right past the family barn. Had a spur built to that barn. The Feds had been trying for years to bust the Pellowskis. We'd sound like hypocrites to our past if we condemned you. We respect yesterday."

I was missing Lulu. Despite her scatterbrained name she was a right smart gal. Kind and generous. Put a beer in her, and soon everyone was laughing and carrying on. She lit up a room. That girl had it, and I was caught up in my way of thinking. Losing the light is what the loss of LuLu meant to me.

Patches hadn't finished with his reminiscing. "The Feds were all over this bar in the day. They'd walk right into this bar, dressed in suits and ties. Sit amongst working farmers. Thinking we were dumb because our clothes were dirty. They stuck out like a sore thumb they did, so nobody told them nothing.

"I should know, being the Pellowskis banked with me. I hired a money guy from Winona to launder the money. Later in his life he ended up being Winona's city treasurer when he got caught laundering city money into his own account."

I looked across the bar and saw Bobby and Dick. Bobby was from over in Waumandee. A good soul with a few marbles loose who made his way to Dodge quite regular to eat the good food and bask in the happiness of everybody knowing his name. Dick was at his annoying best. One of the high-minded Silesian Poles from the town of Arcadia. Good people, sitting around that bar. None too happy with me.

"Success comes to people at all different times, Hanson. Hard work, family, and church bring good fortune. That Arcadia furniture man with all the money was a dirt farming sharecropper from Lewiston. Poor as a person could get. He learned life right early on. His distant relatives came from Second Street in that town you are from. Some mighty wealthy folks in this area all coming from humble roots. Many of them Polish. Hard work, family and church has driven our culture." Patches finished up.

I finished my beer, picked myself up, and decided to take a walk thru old Dodge. See if I could find my dignity. "So long, Patches," I said, as I headed out the back door feeling and hearing that Trempeleau River.

##

I didn't go too far, just out back of the bar. The river was running strong, its sounds releasing me. I lit up a smoke, hoping it would help soothe me. I closed my eyes, letting the sweet sounds of nature calm me.

It's never easy letting go of a relationship. Lulu was a spirit, a soulmate who had been part of my every waking moment for three years. It's sad we couldn't work it out, tried everything but the demons running thru me will wear on anyone. Fly free Lulu. Fly free and find the happiness you deserve.

It's the thing about growing old. Fall asleep at the drop of a hat. I must have been bone tired because when I woke up the sky had grown dark, and some tall old guy was tending a fire near the river.

He looked at me, his eyes piercing the darkness that had fallen. "That Lulu must have been quite the lady. Talking in your sleep. I thought I was the only one did that."

Dodge gets mighty dark at night. Folks not much interested in paying the electric company, but I noticed he was wearing a union jacket and he had a long, white beard.

"I know my face is showing the wear and tear of living," he said as he walked over. He offered his hand and said, "Private George Hoffman. 17th Missouri. Just traveling thru. Got some relatives up the hill in Arcadia that I'm aiming to visit. Anton used to talk about the beauty of this land and its people.

"Anton? You don't have any coffee do you," I asked? I lit up one of my Padolinski cigarettes.

"I got me one of these French Presses. Great for traveling. Living on the road since the war ended. Pehler. Looking for Anton Pehler."

"There's Pehlers in these parts. All over. Why that's their oil company just over the new bridge and a big trucking company up top in Arcadia. Anton, he's of a restless spirit."

He glared at me. "If you fought in that Civil War, you'd be restless too." His arms were gyrating, moving fast in every direction. "Cousins, killing cousins in the backyard of this country. You ever tasted blood you dainty. I ought to break your neck. I ain't slept in my own bed for going on 40 years. Hop a train, walk, eat what I can. This jacket I'm wearing means something. Belittling a brother like you did Anton. I should hang you from that limb above your head."

"I didn't mean nothing by it. Just restless. Couldn't have been easy. Long way from Missouri to the East. Lincoln paid well I hear."

"Not enough. Scarred for life. Better than those confederates who got paid with worthless dollars. Now and then hopping rails, I'll run into a confederate. Good guys mislead by a cause. We share a bottle to forget."

I nodded and told him I had to do my morning thing. Headed down towards the river, letting Mother Nature talk.

##

I came back from my morning duty. It was still early but there were signs of people moving. You could hear doors opening and closing. Dodge was waking up. George had left me a cup of coffee and he had some water boiling over the fire. I had myself a smoke, drank some coffee, and basked in the morning air.

I started thinking about Lulu again. I couldn't get her off my mind when I heard an awful clanking going on behind me.

"Get the hell off my property," someone shouted. The sound of a gun getting ready to shoot came from behind the Kulas Mercantile Store.

"Private First Class George Hoffman," my companion shouted over the clatter.

"You're digging in my garbage. I don't care who you are. What are you doing digging in my garbage for?" The woman's voice lost some of its edge when she saw him better.

"Breakfast, looking for breakfast mixings."

"I got six boys. There isn't anything wasted. I'll give you a piece of bread and some lard. The Kulas family doesn't have table scraps. We work. Wait right here. Don't matter how much I cook, the boys will eat it. All of it. Why didn't you just ask for something?"

George Hoffman straightened up. "Pride. I served in the war. Got sent to Andersonville. Prisoner of War. You get used to bad cooking or no cooking. More than a few of us died from the food. Horrible place. Got treated like dogs. Can't trust what other people are cooking. People trying to kill me. They are coming."

The woman lowered the gun. "Let me get you a cup of water. Sit down. I'll be right back. You don't sound good, and you look like a bag of bones."

"I don't take handouts, Ma'am. It's how I was raised. Besides I wanted soup and that tastes best with scraps. Put some flavor in that river water I'm boiling. I'll go hungry before I take a handout."

"If you walk up to Literski's, I'm guessing they might have some vegetables for your soup. She has got herself a big garden and since their boys moved on they should have some extra food. I sometimes don't know how we are going to put enough food on the table for our boys."

"Thank you but I got myself a bunch of dandelions and some wild asparagus. I'll make do."

"That's fine but if I catch you sniffing around my parts again, I'll shoot and ask questions later."

George had a cross look on his face as he came back to the fire.

Warily, I watched him. He was cussing and swearing, looking this way and that. Staring off into a faraway place. I thanked him for the cup of coffee, and he stared right thru me. I was having a hard time imagining me eating soup with asparagus and dandelion. 'You ain't never been hungry,' I heard my forefathers whisper into my thinking.

Next thing I knew a lady walked right into our camping spot carrying three, dead, cleaned squirrels along with a big frying pan. Started cooking and right behind her came another lady with a bag of vegetables and a big old pork bone.

"I'll fry up this squirrel for you, Private Hoffman," one of them said. "An honor, really. Boys shot them just yesterday. More than willing to help a Veteran who saved this great nation," She shook her head as she talked.

"I got some potatoes and carrots," the other lady said. "I'm Mrs. Kaldunski. I heard there was a veteran visiting our community that was hungry so I ran right over with what I could grab. Can't have a stew without vegetables."

Breakfast was smelling better by the minute. I was hungry and with no Lulu around I was going to have to start feeding myself. George was bent over seemingly in agony. His breathing was short, sporadic and loud. I heard a low sounding eerie cry was coming out of him.

One of the women put a hand on his back. "I'm Mary Wicka. Are you all right, Private Hoffman?"

"They tortured us. No food days on end. We couldn't fight. Weak. People relieving themselves in one corner. Dead people all around us. That stench never leaves you. Thousands in a space for hundreds. Those guards would fry up some meat. Deer from the woods surrounding us. The smell of the grizzled meat filling us. That deer meat never made it to us prisoners. Sheer torture.

"We were animals and they jeered us. Nothing to do but slowly die. I cheered when they hung Wirz who ran the prison. If there's a hell, it got a visitor that day he got hung in Washington." With that he bent over and started shaking.

I looked at Mary. She was speechless. You could feel George and tell something wasn't right.

"What are you staring at?" he roared, staring right at me like he'd never seen me before.

Mary jumped a bit and moved her hand closer to the frying pan and the boiling water. Old George was looking at a hot frying pan if he pushed his luck.

Dodge girls know how to take care of themselves.

##

You could feel them coming over the hill. Everybody leaving church. Coming for their beer. It was Sunday Morning at Hoesley's

Saloon. I was still dealing with George and church had finished 10 minutes ago.

"They noticed you not being at Church this morning," Old Man Kulas said, wandering into the back yard. "Lulu was there, dressed in black. Eyes wearing the dark mascara and her lips painted red-black. Her hair was dyed blonde. That Lulu." He chuckled. "Most folks think you're damn stupid. Walking away from a paying farm. Nuts, I heard more than a few say."

"Why are you telling me that, Mr. Kulas? You think I like losing Lulu's heart? She's a powerful spirit as you well know. Trying to make me feel worse?" I was feeling my Irish rising

I heard my grandfather whispering, "Jab, move, back to the wall. They get ahold of you, and you're done." Dead folk parting wisdom all around me.

"I got a sore aching back from falling asleep out here last night, Mr. Kulas. Exhausted. I miss her. My demons are too much for the good lady to handle. I'm sorry, I'm not wired right. She sure knows how to play a crowd though don't she?"

"You should have seen her. She comes prancing into Church in black like she was mourning. 5 minutes late. Parents in the front row. Young boys turned their heads following her every step. She was playing it for all she was worth. I'm sure some of the boys wished their wives looked like that. Pine Creek-Dodge. No place like it. Even Father Gara paused waiting for her to sit," he chuckled. "She's got a nice walk to her."

He took a seat and continued talking. "You're fortunate. You'd have been the talk of the church social and then the bar social as the parishioners left mass and came to the bars. You can thank Private Hoffman for that. George Hoffman was the talk of the whisperers this morning before church. That's the Pine Creek Band you are hearing. Warming up."

"George don't much like crowds, Mr. Kulas. At least from my sitting, there is something not right with the thinking of Private George Hoffman. Andersonville and too many train rides, he told me this morning. All nerved up. He fidgets around like he's got ants in his pants and his thoughts are all over. Somebody is coming to get him."

"Listen, Hanson, you let Father Gara, know what you're thinking, but if he asks if you want a beer you say 'No,' unless you want the boys mad at you all week. Beer isn't budgeted for and so the boys will have to pay for it next week when he passes the hat. He doesn't buy for just one person. No sir. Everybody gets a beer. Community runs deep in Father Gara."

I took another hit off my smoke and thought what a great little town is Dodge, Wisconsin.

##

Father Gara joined me at the bar and asked about George.

"Well, Father Gara, he went hightailing over the bridge as soon as you all showed up. Singing, horn playing and everybody patting each other on the back. George, he just wants to be left alone. Trying to forget the pain of war. Just as soon be dead. He'll be back, left his traveling bag."

"Surprised he is still around," the good Father said. "Andersonville Prison. A black eye in the history of America. War is man at his worst. Lotta pain lieing in the souls of America. Takes years, generations to let go of the anger, pain. We carry a lot inside us."

"That we do Father. Demons all around. I have to tell you Father. I fell asleep in your church the other night. I slept like a baby. Lulu kicked me out of the house. Nowhere to go."

He looked at me. "The churches doors are always open, Son. Sinners we all are." He paused, looked at me and said, "The dead talk to you?"

"From early on. Shadows early, then the sounds. I ran you know. Took me awhile to realize they weren't so bad. They opened my closed mind."

"You sure you don't have something wrong in your thinking?"

"Probably but I got no juice to fight them anymore. That was a nice body of red wine you had in your confessional booth. Helped me get right to sleep. Your seat cushion sure beat trying to sleep in the hard church pews."

"That was you? I thought maybe I'd finished that wine and

forgot. Sometimes my mind gets going so fast I do forget. It's a blessed bottle so the good Lord's spirit filled you with his blood. Three Hail Mary's for you. Is that your confession?"

"Well, the thing is I must have hit the light switch. It was early when I heard somebody mumbling on the other side of the screen.

"Bless me Father for I have sinned," she started up. "My last confession was two days ago."

"I was trapped so I gave my best Latin. "E Pluribis Unum. Dolce Dolte. She was a widow she told me and Leonard had just lost his wife across the way. She said she felt an urge, an attraction to Leonard. Lust one of the deadly sins you know she said, and asked me for forgiveness. I told her two rosaries and she could bring Leonard a fresh baked pie."

He started laughing. A drink for everyone he roared, and all the church elders gave me dirty look. Kulas, Losinski, and Lipinski all stared at me, forever counting their pennies as Father Gara roared Na Zdrobia at the top of his lungs. He leaned over and whispered to me. "I'll talk to George Hoesley and see if we can put him up in the Hoesley Hotel for the night. A man deserves a good night's sleep." And the beer tasted fine as the money counters grumbled.

##

We finally reached Harry's Place, in the unincorporated town of Pine Creek, Wisconsin.

Now Harry and I hadn't seen each other in 40 years so we looked at each other from a couple different directions before we remembered what we looked like in those innocent years. When I told him I'd been talking to the dead his eyes lit up like a Christmas tree.

"Me too," he said.

I was drinking a sapphire and tonic in a big plastic cup. I had bought Science Girl one as well. Seven bucks for two drinks and a Sprite.

The place was nothing more than a square box. A hot tub and a deck out back but it was filled with people laughing and carrying on. Harry's Place is one of those must stops if you get off the beaten path enough to get to Pine Creek.

##

"If you ain't a sight for sore, tired eyes. Never thought I'd get to talk to a real live human being. Father Gara, he never said anything about afterlife being like this." Then he laughed, a deep throated laugh from the heart which told me a great deal about Jacob Pellowski.

I was road tripping thru Pine Creek and Dodge with the Polish Collaborative and I don't think Anne, Frank, Beef, Father Dernek, Charley and Joe heard the voices of Mr. and Mrs. Jacob Pellowski like I did.

We made it to Pine Creek, stopping at the cemetery like good Polish folk. All the familiar names. Took the short cut from Pine Creek to Dodge to the Pellowski home.

I heard Mrs. Pellowski, soon as we stepped out of the car, whisper to me, that its pronounced *Pellofski*. If you are going to write about us Kashubians get it right. My maiden name was Zabinski and I was born in 1863 right in Winona. It was here on this porch that Jacob cut the deal with the Chicago families. We made the shine by the barrel and being the train ran along the back 40 it was easy to distribute. Stopped every day until it didn't no more. We weren't hurting nobody. It was just moonshine. Hanson, I want to introduce you to my husband Jacob. You notice he wears a metal brace on his leg. 1916 milling accident. The saw got him. Hard on him and the family. Jacob didn't like not being able to work like he once did. It was his value, understand? He sat on this porch doing some brooding. Lived over twenty years with half a leg. But his darkest moment was when his son, Alex, got sent to jail."

"Hanson, a pleasure to meet you," he said. He was a large man with big hands used to working. Farm hands. I was born on the boat ride over. 1859. My brother Alex died at the age of one on the same creaky boat. Buried at sea somewhere in the deep Atlantic. Ma told me it was hard leaving all we knew. Grandparents from a long ways back. I named my son after my brother.

"Those Chicago boys couldn't go anywhere without their flashy cars, suits and guns. Greased back hair. Tried telling them they stuck out like a sore thumb in these parts but there was no changing them. Violent, you could just feel their violence that they had running thru them. They treated us good. Ma didn't like them. She had a healthy distrust of most outsiders. She'd get a going you know. She didn't like their suits and slicked back hair. They drove their fancy automobiles right out to the farm. All the neighbors talked amongst themselves . They all had stills but we had the railroad tracks running right next to the farm. Us Polish stuck together."

I noticed Father Richard looking at me

Joe said, "Let's drive over to the barn where the brewing was done."

Mr and Mrs. Pellowski waved and I heard them say we'll see you at the Stockyard.

Winona Wanderings

I like the night, the darkness, the feeling that comes over me as the rest of town sleeps. I breathe deep breaths not smelling the car exhaust for they too are resting. The college students and second shifters tucked away for the night. Bars closed and I can see yesterday.

I was sitting across from the courthouse enjoying a smoke and a bottle of wine, hearing that old building talking like old buildings do.

"We changed people and life," it roared, and I remembered my time in a courthouse when my life changed. Two court houses, different places, designed by the same man. Winona architect, CJ Maybury.

That Court house sings. Folks whispering their stories. I can hear when the lights of the world get turned off. Noise, noise all around me blocking that path to that other side.

One voice stood out. "It was the last taste of freedom I ever had that courthouse was. Guilty not denying that. Trapped in the thralls of alcohol. I would've drunk anything. Trying to kill myself, I was. Couldn't shake the craving. I remember the day after waking up in the morning, hungover and not thinking clearly.

"I shot a man at 2nd and Main. A hotel for the Indigent. He denied me a whiskey. I killed him. The rest of my life I spent behind bars. I just wanted a drink. No excuses. Poor, homeless, no hope, no future. I was a bum traveling through. I could hear my heart beating when the gavel came down," he said.

I took another hit and a large swig of the wine, breathing. Seeing that tall courthouse in the light of its time. I felt another person, a woman, beside me.

Her voice was wistful. "I was elated when Lawyer Libera became a judge, thinking us Polish people had a voice in the courts. And when he finally became Judge, we thought we had risen from our humble beginnings. We had, but Judge Libera gave us no breaks. If the Devil's seeds had filled our sons with such force that our church and our Babushkas couldn't straighten them out, Judge Libera would sentence them hard. The Army or Jail he was known to rule, and that drill Sargent often did what the church and family couldn't," she said.

Some of the finest lawyers in the country have practiced their craft in the courthouse that was like a second office. Deep pockets have long known the best lawyers win and the little guy gets trampled fighting for his or her justice. Still that way today as money rules the roost.

Maybury was the architect of the times. He was the architect on the Windom house redo, and he designed the houses that the Mayo Brothers of Rochester lived in. He built the church that towers over the East End and the Central Methodist church too. Many buildings built by the man who came to Winona with a hammer and a dream with a gift of drawing.

I sat on the bench in front of the Redman's Club. The sun was rising, and I headed home.

##

I was out sharing a smoke with Petey Hawaiian, behind the Labor Temple sharing laughs and carrying on. The North Country Band was playing, and the pretty girls were all dancing. Petey was telling me about this red bud which caused a person and his thinking to go haywire in a different way.

"Here, inhale this and you'll find your mind in a different place, a different time. Those Hippie boys and gals tell me this red bud, is the devil's weed. You'll be asking questions. You'll never think the same as you dance with the devil's weed. You won't know who you are as that weed takes root. Take right over your soul," he said. "Coats it with love, brother."

Now Petey never mislead me before and sure enough the red bud began working its magic. We shared a hit and I started walking the dark downtown alleys. The red bud started talking, asking who I was and what mattered. I shook my head as those voices peppered me with questions. What lay at the heart of man the red bud asked? I kept a moving, figuring it is harder to hit a moving target.

By the time I crossed Market Street, past the old VFW, now called Market Tap, I was seeing different. I could hear the grand old bar calling, but I carried on, mostly afraid of having to talk with the living. The shadows whispered, and old vets were sharing stories about lives left on the battlefields of foreign wars. Old friends, sharing life's meaning over a smoke and a beer. Life, a moving target to the understanding as I smiled at finding the wisdom the red bud brought to my being.

"Forgiveness," I heard the god whisper. "The fixer of all that ails."

"The souls of man, my stock and trade," the Devil man chortled. "Seeds of the devil bring the fruit you all want. You hear those seven deadly sins ringing through your soul as you eat my deadly fruit. They exist in every one of you living."

"I've sat in many a pew, stared out many a stained glass," I said. I heard the Nighthawks perched on the high points of buildings surveying the town they once looked over. I felt the devil hanging, just waiting to pounce on the thoughts swirling inside my head.

I took another hit as I heard my Marine Daddy yell charge. I told the devil man I was one step in front as I heard my Irish ancestors raise a glass and a yell. I turned to the proud warriors asking them, "What it is you are tempting me with?" Then I heard a yell coming from down the alley.

"Hanson, Hanson I got a fixing. Come enter my den. Let's sit and talk. Just you and me."

##

When they are gone, they are gone. When the bricks get taken down or the skies of Winona get lit up a part of us dies. The old brick building down by the tracks and levee was one of those buildings.

A great family once operated their business in the back part of that building, grew into it, and out of its functional usage. Like so many others, they became a global corporation, and their plant is now a low-slung plant down in the far east end.

But when that building gets taken down one of the visual reminders of a great company will be no more. We won't see that reminder, that name downtown. Just a name on a building can trigger a kid and his thinking, his interests. Family drives don't happen like they used to and getting a kid to wonder about a company by the name of Peerless Chain and the four brothers who started it isn't a bad thing.

Those old brick buildings were part of our growing up. We didn't know anything, thought we knew it all, but even today I can't shake Winona. Sticks with me like glue so when Cheryl and I go visit a town or get away for a weekend we stay, we eat, and we buy downtown. We enjoy downtown, and we drive through places where old buildings stand. I can't feel the dead in the suburbs.

Something about that river has made for some prosperous folks. John Latsch, used to tie his canoe somewhere along the levee. Joseph Bambenek and his brothers stared out at that river figuring out how to expand their chain market most efficiently. Fastenal and its early roots started there too. Probably not a living person amongst us who ever tasted the brew that was made there and shut down by prohibition. The recipe probably lost, tossed, thrown away and burned. Time has a way of stopping along the river.

That river can talk, lighting up a person's thinking. Bernie Rothwell bought a burnt-out mill down by the river. The place had been gutted by fire and the 1893 financial panic, out from a bankruptcy of Mr. Porter, an early Winona businessman. Mr. Rothwell and his family have taken that stake and turned it into a multi-plant business operation and the Porter Mill became Bay State Milling with their huge silos down by the river.

Now that brick building isn't the prettiest but if you take a good long look that gal talks yesterday. That building had heart and the men and women who worked there shared that heart. She stares at you, and you wonder what she is about. She ain't get no fancy pedigree, but that girl worked, and hard work has long defined this town. We all don't look at buildings the same.

##

I sat down on the bright orange red chairs outside of Yarnology on Third street in downtown Winona. It was one of those days where my body had no get up and go. Plumb didn't want to go anywhere, do anything. Just sit.

Luscious sat beside me and started talking. "The winds of change blowing through our living Hanson. Can't you see it in the skies, the trees and the way people walk and talk to each other. It's a slow-moving storm, yes sir, working its way through us, something just ain't quite right in all that's going on."

Luscious lived in a small apartment above the stores in downtown Winona. She might have worked the Kresge's counter or The Steak Shop or been a friend of Jeannie Lebeau down at the Hurry Back. Never asked her, didn't know, nor care, how she got where she was.

Growing up in Winona, watching Third Street through the years, was like a side show at the carnival with all sorts of oddities passing by. Thank you, thank you, thank you, I say to all the people of my past.

Mr. Commerce man, walked past, all sparkly and dazzling, wearing a fine suit and sporting a cane which seemed to have no function except for being stylish. "Winona has a proud tradition of being a hard-working town," he said. "A unique combination of brains, brawn and deep pockets has allowed this wonderful river town to prosper since its inception. Put that in your story Hanson," he said.

I looked at Luscious. I could tell she wasn't seeing nor hearing what the polished man was saying. I suppose, like most, loneliness got to Luscious through time, set right in her bones as she saw how she was the only person listening to her thoughts and words. She was paying no attention to much of anything except the narrative running through her own skull. All her friends were dead and not a soul knew her story.

Now Mr. Commerce he had a high sense of himself. That energy running through him made a person sit up and notice, and he expected to be heeded. "My name Is Hannibal Choate," he said. He was ram rod straight with a sharpness to his features and a long nose. "I was the President of Choate's Department Store and Merchants Bank. You know what's wrong with your generation, Hanson? You live too much inside your head, exercising the wrong part of your thinking. You don't question, you don't pause before jumping. The essentials of living. Prosperity comes from questioning, searching for a better tomorrow."

I just let Mr. Hannibal rant. Seems I've surrounded myself with ranters in that world of the disease which occupies my thinking. We all got crutches and those voices swirling inside me let me cope with the non-stop sounds of present day living.

He stared at me and said he was old enough to remember the Civil War. He kept a map in his store down there on second, at his first store before he built the big one that stands as a testament to the American way. I wasn't sure he and I carried the same meaning of the American way, but I was sick and didn't care to argue. He kept on a ranting about how he had newspapers brought to his door from all parts of the country just so he could track the war movements.

I asked him how getting week-old or even older papers gave him any accuracy.

He said, "The key to a successful businessman is seeing patterns. There were only so many roads to travel down so you could get a pretty good idea where folks were headed next and where forces down the road would bump heads. The talk of the town was all about the war. Nothing much else mattered, and I sold supplies to the thousands of people who traveled to Winona looking for jobs and seeking fortune. They spoke in the tongue of their native land when excited. They carried stories about where they were from and the hearings and sights of a country at war.

"Everybody knew I had a large map on wall down at the store which showed where the troops were to the best of our guessing, and because my maps were the finest and most accurate known we could track the wars progress quite well. Only so many ways into and out of Gettysburg and all signs were pointing to a meeting of opposing forces a few weeks before the fighting began. Our boys serving were part of Company K, Hanson. Winona, Southeastern Minnesota, and the boys were by all accounts waiting at Gettysburg for history to happen. Those letters the boys sent to their mothers brought tears to those who read.

"Our town was worried, Hanson. The young men of our country were part of Company K. Yes, that Company K who gave up their lives to stop Lee. Robert E. Lee at Cemetery Ridge. When they cut Lee off, they had to know they were dead before they ran across the field. That Captain Cowell from Red Wing had to send our boys dying to their early graves. Our boys gave up their lives to keep the union together and I hope their last vision before seeing the holy light was seeing Lee hightail his way back South.

"We could tell a couple weeks before that a battle was brewing at Gettysburg as troops from both sides seemed to be moving into place. We figured Lee was trying to circle DC. I mean us old Winona boys knew well Sam Whiting, the captain of the Marion who picked up the wives, children and soldiers of Fort Sumter. He refused to dip the American Flag to the bombastic bantam roosters of South Carolina. Made Winona proud. We've always marched to our own drummer, Hanson. Captain Sam was the editor of a couple early Winona newspapers."

I stared ahead sizing up the block of my youth. Ted Maier and Grants, Woolworths and St. Clairs and down there on the corner where Blooming Grounds stands was once a waterbed store and a post office as history unfolded right before my eyes.

"Hanson, did you know Mugsy Bates died," Luscious asked, interrupting Mr. Choate. "He and I had shared a morning of beers down at the Eagles just last week. He had to know he was dying and nary a word of impending death. He entered the great beyond without blinking an eye. With all the bad things that had fallen upon

Mugsy while living I sure hope he was met at the gate with welcoming arms and a cold, cold beer as life evened out."

I thought of all the interesting people I've met sitting on a bench, staring up at buildings that had a way of talking to me. Finding yesterday like it was today and thinking what a great life I've had.

##

"I knew Johnny Latsch. He was no normal man. No, he didn't carry any of that Victorian pomposity in him that gripped many of the deep pockets. He had a quirk to his thinking, his talking. He could talk to anyone and did. Had a memory like an elephant."

I was sitting on the stoop of Beno's Deli waiting for my takeout.

Ezra stood in front of me. He was disheveled with an overgrown mustache. He was missing a few teeth and his eyes twinkled. He told me he'd has spent a few nights in the jail that used to be above Beno's Deli. "This was the City Hall, Jailhouse and everything that had to do with local governance. Miss Corrine cooked for us jailbirds."

He was talking as he was drinking out of the brown paper bag, so his words sometimes slurred. "To the day I don't know how she fed us on the pennies she was given to feed us. We were mostly boys who drank too much except for Betty Big Bottom. She'd be right in the middle of the biggest fights.

"We just got drunk and unruly. Our townie heart beats boom town and all the things that come with that. The boys who carried Billy clubs would bang us on the head and round us up. My cousin Nob, the cop, whacked me on the head more than a few times.

"Now you got to remember that the lumber mills had moved their operations west. We elected John Latsch Jr. mayor, because he gave us hope. We were worried. The East enders voted for the man whose parents were Swiss, as the lumber industry which brought us here said goodbye. The money stayed here a good long while the workers raised their families and made their money in a faraway state named Washington."

I asked Miss Corrine how she became such a good cook and

she started talking about Mrs. Fockens who was the cook at the Arlington Club which is now the parking lot next to Bub's. She cooked for two Presidents, William Taft and Warren Harding. A kind, kind lady who, like most folks, didn't have a pot to pee in. She lived down on East Second with her family. She was upstairs and they were down.

Winona has never been wasteful and so Mrs. Fockens would send the jail her excess food rather than throw it. Then she whispered that Master Li at the Chinese laundromat on the second floor of Bub's sold oriental spices that made food come alive. Spices.

Ezra said it was time to leave, and I looked up and down the street feeling yesterday. I took a deep breath and thought what a great country we live in as I stood, walked inside Beno's and got my sandwich.

##

Lotta change coming to our river town. Winona people don't much like change. Keep it the way it is I hear them cry.

I stopped at Sammy's to pick up my sausage, mushroom, extra cheese pizza after looking at our empty downtown storefronts. I see cars and people walking. Their noses in their smart phones, mostly ignoring the history all around them as if the buildings didn't talk. Build an App.

Pretty soon we'll have bicyclists filling our streets as our town gets connected to the bike trails of Wisconsin. And those Wisconsin folks are making it happen. Seems like the bike path gets built as spring springs.

Those bicyclists drop money as they go about their recreation. Some are day trippers while others will spend the night and eat good foods, listen to good music.

Where they will stay and where will they park and where will they ride their bikes in this beautiful town between the bluffs and along the river? But they are not the only ones bringing change to a town whose roads were built for and in older times.

Fastenal will be building a beautiful corporate headquarters on the land where Charlie's once stood. The boys in the big electric trucks have been doing their thing getting everything ready for the 300 people a day who will make it their office. And with it will come how many hundreds more all looking to partner with the Fastenal brand? All coming downtown. Cars everywhere, moving slowly, looking to park, stopping and starting.

Changing dynamics coming to our town, I thought as I took my first bite. Still hot and I could stretch that wonderful cheese. I was eating down at the Levee, being the Covid had shut down the Port 507. Beer and pizza go together and though Sammy's serves beer in these beautiful days of late spring, I like being outside, and drinking at the Levee is no longer allowed.

We are fortunate Mr. Kierlin and his partners are building a beautiful building which will enhance our once great downtown. If the building put up on the parking lot that was Hardee's is any indicator, Winona should take pride in the building whose fortune lay in nuts and bolts and delivering them to people when they need them. The folks living in the apartments drive cars and the businesses on the ground floor need places for their customers to park.

The pizza was hitting the spot as I wondered about the cluster that was going to snarl traffic into and out of Winona. In a manufacturing town, starting and stopping is not how product flows best.

So little land in this town divided by railroad tracks. So much fear of changing times. Thinking status quo isn't fixing the problem about to happen in the streets of a quiet river town. I took my last bite and went searching for a beer.

##

I took a sip of my absinthe. The room was spinning. My eyes were seeing faint images and I hear people laughing and talking. Old soldiers and grand dames talking yesterday.

The music of the times was bouncing off the walls. Big Band, Country, Rock and the Blues. A lonely Sax played. Alone I felt as the absinthe worked through me.

Shorty Bags was on my left whispering about how his pecker don't work no more and his girl was getting ready to leave him. I didn't feel like listening to that country song, so I turned to the tall, thin guy on my right telling me he made his way hearing the confessions of us townies. I looked at him; he was bony, tall, and bent as if the worries of the world had fallen upon on his shoulders.

He kinda stuttered. "You, you young people have stopped hearing. Tone deaf. Running around like a chicken with your head cut off. It happens, you got that TV, and the pretty faces are loud, bold, flashy, glitzy. Flash sells. You've lost your focus, your identity. You don't have a chance, your world is filled with too much sound, not enough quiet in your thinking.

"You know what I liked about this town, Hanson? I certainly wasn't the same priest at 34 that I was at 64. As a young man I thought the world could be easily fixed with right and wrong. God's right and wrong as said in the book was the fix, but as I sat in that confessional booth and heard the tales of darkness, I questioned. We were like star dust sprinkled randomly from the skies above and as that star dust, that carbon, settled life began."

I looked at him. His eyes were of a different place, and he carried on.

"I lost confidence in my early believing. Life had weighed in. Doubt crept into my thinking about the origins, the origins of it all."

I hear the sound of a church organ weighing in on his standings as the absinthe hit my bones. Judge Challeen was looking at me with the quiet raised eyebrow that said careful from the end of the horseshoe bar end where he was sitting. I asked for a Coke.

"I was doing confessions up there at the school on the hill. They were mostly rich kids. Many were sent to get their heads on straight. Anyway, the brothers required that they give their confession once a week.

"I got bored. All they talked about was wanting to meet those St. Theresa gals. I used to get mad, yelling and screaming mad as they talked of their fantasies. Perhaps it was my own sexually repressed fantasies coming out in a different way. That's when I learned they were playing me, trying to get me to snap.

"There was a betting pool you see. Whose confession would cause me to start yelling and screaming won the cash. They drew numbers as to who went first. I look back and say well played, well played and I never screamed again. This is a great town, a great town Hanson."

##

I was walking west Third on the block where the Snack Shop and the Riverbed Cafe used to call home. It was the weekend of the Midwest Music Fest, the opening of Winona's summer. Thousands of musicians and their fans were supposed to descend upon our fair city, spending thousands and creating memories that last a lifetime.

"Hanson, you'd have liked this block. The walls talked, the buildings talked, and it was an era where people talked. This was my shop and I lived upstairs. Never paid full price for anything. Wasn't a new thing in my store.

"Rickety old buildings that told stories. Now we got a phone company building, taking up a quarter of the block and operating out of a building that looks like the architecture of the Soviet Union. Progress, hardly. Got to cross the street to get a beer!

"Every evening I'd sit right outside my store. People out walking everywhere. Some of them buying, some not. People gathering for the sake of gathering. That Hurry Back was a hopping place. Kids all over what with the school downtown. You even saw cops walking the beat. Downtown Winona was quite the place.

"When the Huff Hotel was still standing you never saw such an odd mix of characters mingling together. Big city folks hobnobbing with us River Folk. People would come back year after years telling me that a person could relax here. Entertainment every night when the Opera House brought in their vaudeville act and the wrestling matches held at the Armory sold out.

"I had the best seat in the house to the splendor that is Winona's history," she said. "I met them all from the pool hustlers at the Hurry Back to the bastard Henry Huff. So many interesting people have been through this town, down this street.

"I remember Mr. Norton of Laird, Norton came into the store. I recognized him. Then he started talking and his voice was not harsh and mean but gentle, kind and caring. He was heartbroken and it showed in his eyes and gloomy complexion. He told me of his first son's dying.

"Broke my heart. The pain of a dead child. 'My son was in

Boston,' he said. 'Learning about the world. Going to run the lumber company as I slowly stepped back from the day to day. We got a wire that he was gravely sick. Gone before we could hop a train and get to Boston.' Then quiet. He just shook his head and said he would have his driver Henry drop off his son Matthew's clothes."

She was wearing a dark green Robin Hood style hat with a pink feather. Matching pink cowboy boots and a multi-colored skirt covering the top of her boots.

"You look marvelous," I said, and her eyes watered as she told me of yesterday.

"I heard us dead folk can talk to you. Didn't believe it when I first heard about your knack."

I was having a cup of coffee in the Riverbend café. Jenny was waitressing. She looked at me with concern.

"Tough night?"

"All around me. Not looking good today either. Must be spring. Everywhere I turn."

She shook her head as she walked away. Dudley was cooking and the smells of good food filled the air. I was sitting with Louise.

"It's one of the things you miss when you step on over. Coffee in the morning. Sharing a space with all the walks of life. Community you know. Nobody knows us anymore. You don't even know yourselves. You young folks have lost your identity," the old dame said.

"That's kind of damning to us younger folk," I replied. "The seeds of our problems have been festering for a good long while."

I was recovering from a night of whiskey and listening to Tobasco Cat. The tones of time talking as I slowly woke. My world was crumbling. The things I believed in were falling apart. Dark clouds all around me as the voices raged thru my head. The devil and St. Michael, dueling swords. Good and Evil slaying the things I believed in. Stomping on the ways of my thinking.

That separation of mind, Schizophrenia, as the word means, was running wild. A devil's seed, my creek clan was saying. They worried about the devil, knowing how that devil feasted on minds. The devil's seeds bearing fruit, falling to rest as life does. The tooth can run a bit long in the parts of the town where I got roots.

"That Devil, will be taking over your thinking," the whispers said. "That Devil will get you all twisted inside out, upside down. Twist your soul as the Devil wears camouflage.

"We are here." More voices whispered. "We live in the caverns, the deepest parts of your mind. We come out triggered by words and actions. We like you angry, we like you mad. Fruit blossoming. The Devil's delight."

The chants of the devil shared my morning cup. "Have to walk my path to really see who is evil and good," they whispered. From all sides the voices come. I gulped my coffee just trying to keep one foot in front of the Devil as he practiced his ancient craft.

The soft melodies of the piano tumbled through my thoughts, triggering the voices of my conscience as they raged from deep within. Jay was playing that keyboard lightly on that old piano sitting in the back of the cafe as I sat talking to voices rattling inside my thinking. Cup after cup.

I could feel the devils brew churning inside me. That Good/Evil complex that churchmen weave being tested by questions as time reveals.

Old coaches yell, "What are you made of?" Uncle Wayne says face up and Dad, the old Marine calls for a charging up that hill, never halfway as the marine heart gets fulfilled and I tumbled into the world of my insanity.

I walked outside. I could smell grizzled meat coming from Clancy's Restaurant in the basement of the Morgan Block across the street and all that coffee was wearing a hole in my stomach. I was always hungry in those days of yesterday and not hardly any money in my pocket.

Downtown had a buzz to it. As a young man the migration to Highway 61 had begun. Randall's, Tempo, Montgomery Ward, and a string of franchised corporate stores. The High School became a Jr. High and eventually some nice apartments. Our small library remains and fond memories of the children's library run through us.

I always liked walking amongst the brick buildings of downtown. I'm not looking to buy, but I always find something on the way. I walk past the Watkins Bank and think of my days sitting in the church pew and hearing money doesn't buy happiness as I recall the Watkins nephew and his death at the Princeton Hotel.

I see the new post office and think of the old and the park where Mr. Landon commissioned a sculpture of Princess Winona for his wife which now sits in Windom Park. The old Landon Home stood where the Winona National Bank drive-thru is.

I see the old houses where the YWCA once stood and now houses an Autism Center and I remember the strong, strong women who walk and walked the streets of this town. Their lumber money worked behind the scenes in the male culture of the times as the moneyed boys seemed better at making girls who chose husbands to run the companies their fathers founded.

I turn to see the new face on the block. Rising up on a block which once housed a YMCA, Livery Stable, Cable TV office, a car dealership called Owl Motor and Chrysler Corner. Hardees. I see this beautiful building, its lines, its length and thought to myself what a wonderful addition to a great town as the voices of my schizophrenia start whispering well done, Bob. Well done, Mr. Kierlin.

##

I was having coffee at the Sicilian Bakery located between Doc Tabor's orthodontist office and the Winona Clinic, facing Winona National Bank. I was having a cannolli with my coffee when the old guy showed up. I had been searching for the old man.

"Death is going to get you sure as the sun sets every evening. It caught me in 1899. All my friends raised a glass when my death was announced. None of us realized we'd ever get a chance to talk again."

I looked at the old white-haired man. He talked with a southern accent. He was dressed in an old dusty, stuffy suit with a bow tie.

"My name is Francis Cockrell," he said. "Most folks called me Colonel and I was a Southern Gentleman. I was the owner of the Huff Hotel located where the Kensington sits.

"Henry Huff, a scoundrel befitting the times, had built it. He built it with no interest in running it. My partner and I bought out Mr. Willis, the first proprietor, shortly after our arrival in Winona in those days before the Civil War.

"Winona was a boom town back then. Lumber, wheat, railroads. Free land and immigrants chasing freedom, unheard of in the old country. Our town was full of people speaking in different tongues and free land. People just wanting a chance to control their own destiny. We hale from Europe where Kings reigned upon our ways of life.

"I was a Southerner surrounded by Yankees. Kentucky bred and I kept maps on the wall as we followed troop movements between North and South as close as we could during the war down at the old Huff Hotel.

"We got all the newspapers, and we saw Gettysburg happening a couple weeks out. The eastern newspapers had reporters on the front lines. Newspapers coming from all over this country to the Huff Hotel."

"Colonel Cockrell," I said. "You lived in the white house on the corner of 4th and Johnson; the one that got tore down and became the Winona Opera House and eventually a parking lot. Rocco's Pizza was across the street. You lived there with your two spinster sisters, and Lena."

"That's right. A day doesn't pass without my thinking of Lena. Tom Williams and I hired her in 1858 to do the laundry," Cockrell said. "It wasn't long before she was running the entire operation. My life changed you see. She took care of my every need.

"I was a socializer. Drinking got to me. If it hadn't been for Lena I don't know if I could have run the Huff Hotel. One night Tom and I got in a heated argument. The whole bar heard us going at it and during a drunken rage I told him I was going to kill him. Dumb, dumb, dumb.

"A week later Tom met his death. He was trying to do some mechanical work on a gas line and an explosion occurred. Dead. His face and body mangled. People looked away when they saw me coming believing I killed my partner. Words weighing on the minds of those all around me.

"I had nothing to do with Tom and his dying just a drunken

rant. It didn't matter to Lena, and I wonder today if Lena's loyalty to me had caused Tom's dying. Everyone thought I was guilty. Lena held the wake on the second floor of the Hotel and all the employees attended. It was an open casket and Tom's head was a mangled mess.

She'd a done anything for me. It's why she lays with me at the cemetery. Ain't no way she would have killed herself. I couldn't bear to ask her if she done killed Tom, but I know someone killed her."

##

"The stains of battle, bloody scars were part of me. My Grandfather was an officer in the Revolutionary war and I had uncles fight and die in that war of 1812. War and killing turns a man ugly.

"I remember as a small child, Reverend Silas would get too preaching, preaching on the Pulpit that killing was the fruit of the Devils seed and that it doesn't stop with the act.

"You can taste war. It gets in your mind, that Devils fruit; it'll grab your heart. Crawl right inside your skin, the smell of blood it doesn't leave you," he'd get to screaming.

"Thou shall not kill! The devil is preying on man and he would point upwards to the Lord himself. Reverend Silas had this white beard that stretched down to his chest, kinda frizzy. No Hair, he had no hair on top and his eyes looked cross, mean. He wore a tall hat when he wasn't preaching, and the old folks whispered don't cross his path. He carries a whip in his words. Hell awaits."

"I knew killing sat in every church pew being it was my kin and as a young man I couldn't wait to leave those Kentucky hills where grudges last forever, getting nowhere but deeper."

"You told stories Colonel Cockerel," I said.

"Ain't nothing like a Southern storyteller," he said as I finished my second cannolli, savoring its last bite. The block had changed. Gone was the grand Post Office, Togs 'N Toys, a Bank that bought the assets of another Bank that housed the lumber and railroad fortunes of a different era. Landon's mansion gone as time flew. What a grand, grand city this was. I sipped my coffee slowly.

##

I headed to the Levee. Colonel Cockrell had told me if I wanted to really know Lena Weinberg, I should head down to Second. It was the heart and soul of Winona he said.

I left the bakery, walking past the new Winona Clinic. I saw a parking lot where a once great post office stood. I waved at Chinky Deerman, sitting in the shades of its shadows. Now, like then, I kept my distance. I waved at Nola in her bright colored shop as I made my way.

Owl Man sat in his antique shop counting time, collecting yesterday. Erberts and Gerberts stands where Shotgun Sersha had his General Store. A California drive thru bank now stands where the Salvation Army and the Riverbend Cafe once stood. Progress is hard on the memories.

Gone were the two-story brick buildings that made up the Morgan Block. I yearn for the smell of grizzled meat and fried onions that used to come from Clancy's and Barney's, where the owner cooked food, raised a family, and paid his bills.

I sat down on a bench looking at how time had wielded its sword when I felt a purse whack me aside the head.

"Lena Weinberg, was one of the finest persons to ever walk these streets of Winona," the woman said. "She stood up for regular folk who did what we had to do to survive. Lena didn't kill herself: she fought for us till the day she died. She was murdered."

I didn't say much. All my years of training told me not to add fuel to the fire.

"We had nowhere to go," she said. "The Civil War had wiped out a generation of young men. There was no safety net. Work or die, work harder or live like animals. I sold my body but never my soul. Lena nourished me on dark days.

"Lena used to walk the streets every morning, picking up news as she went. If a man treated one of us poorly, he was paid a visit and told not to visit again. Move along she said, or the catfish will get supper.

"We used to drink coffee at a place called the Dew Drop Inn. Best coffee in town. Tilly only used the Bell Lard made right down there in the East End on the land that Peerless Chain sits today. Swift had the plant that used to be called the Interstate Packing Company.

Butchered hogs and cows, doing business until 1965."

Tilly must have been seventy and she was slowing down. Her husband, Sy, couldn't hardly move no more. He had tried wiring a new outlet for Tilly and zapped himself right good. Told him in no uncertain terms that drinking and electrical work didn't work together. Sy just had his own way of thinking.

Second Street from early on was a world upon itself. You could get an education just by walking down Second. When steamboats and trains dropped off passengers and products for living, Second Street was like a jolt of lightning in a town that worked hard. Not everybody frequented those upstairs rooms. There wasn't a finer place to people watch. Winona had its roots on second.

"Lena had enemies," she said as she left.

##

"I was a kid. Too young to serve. Eight years old. Summer of 1863." The voice started out shaky.

I was behind the John Latsch building on Second. It was a dark alley. The space behind the building and the tracks. A nice amble down to the river before the floods of the 60's. I was sitting on the loading dock. Just a single light overhead. The voices were running wild, and I was having a smoke trying to settle them.

"On July 4th of 1863, I had a shovel in my hands and was burying dead soldiers under a hot, sticky July sun. I was a child of Gettysburg. Just a kid tasting death. My reality, Hanson."

I felt myself relaxing. The thousand voices had become one. I could breathe.

"On July 4, 1863 I lost my childhood. Taken before I was ready. Not that I would have amounted to much. Daddy was a drunk and we weren't quite sure where he was. Mama got herself a bad case of the flu. She was dead in three months. I think it was the smells of the dead that triggered her dying. I came to Winona in 1864.

"Latsch Sr. gave me a job. Sweeping, dusting, doing anything needed doing. He was a hard man. He had a mangled arm, and he took it out on everyone he came across. He ruled with an iron fist, and he seemed to enjoy inflicting hardship.

"He left me alone. I worked hard. Didn't talk much. Mrs. Latsch once told me Sr. left me alone because I was of the walking dead. The haunting of Gettysburg was what I carried everywhere I went. I wasn't alone. The entire country carried the scars of the uncivil war.

"So many flies. Thousands upon thousands feasting on dead remains. Horses and men. Where all those flies came from, we didn't know but they came in swarms. Vultures and crows filling the skies looking for dinner.

"It was terrifying, I was just a kid. The sounds of guns echoing. Our little bitty town was never the same. We used to run thru the killing fields. The fields of our innocence. Children didn't run in the fields anymore after all the killing. Cemetery Ridge, where the First Minnesota took its last breath was the field of my youth.

"The memories of the longest day of my life get triggered on July 4th. That day never ended. The thoughts of Gettysburg rattled inside my brain till my dying. Then finding the hereafter. You don't shake what I saw. I went from being a kid trying to learn to smoke to a kid carrying amputated body parts and burying them. A matter of days."

##

It was the end of a nice Winona summer day. The sun had found itself setting in the western sky. The sky was a beautiful orange and I felt my roots talking. Science Girl and I were headed to the Athletic Club to listen to the comforting sounds of the Bus Boys. Mark, Wayne and Dedrick.

The Athletic Club is a bar where a man can breathe. In no time at all I felt surrounded by the voices of yesterday. I saw Doris and Eddie Gryzbowski talking kindly to anyone who walked by. A good time by all.

I felt him before I saw him; he looked like a wreck. Blood shot eyes, disheveled hair and half an ear gone.

"Joseph Knitter. My name is Joseph Knitter. I've been dead a good long while. The last years of my life were wasted. Not remembered. Early years too. It was the only thing I was good at. Drinking, that is," he snarled. "I threatened my wife with an ax and bloodied her nose and eyes with my fists. Not once, twice but near every day. Still don't know why she didn't leave me. Judge Tawny ordered the bars to not serve me. I was a drunk who used to work for the Milwaukee Railroad. My name was a regular in the Winona Republican Herald. I killed my wife and our baby. I beat on her pregnant stomach and her angelic face."

"What happened to your ear?" I asked. His was a hard story to hear.

"Bartholomew Sopa is what happened. Can't even tell you what we were fighting about but every time we ran into each other a fight ensued. He might have ate it for all I know. Miserable bastard.

"My life was a mess. I had three children that got sent to orphanages in Detroit after Mrs. Knitter died. That's the last I heard. I was dead a few years later. Train ran me over. Middle of nowhere. Up by Minnieska, when the road was a trail.

"I used to drink in Strehlow's Park that was the land the Athletic Club sits on. People need to gather, rub shoulders, talk to different folks whether it's Strehlow's Beer Garden, The Hurry Back, The Athletic Club or that Peter's Biergarten downtown. We built campfires and shared stories down east here.

##

The Hurry Back had a long history in this town. It was founded by a man named Putnam right around the turn of the century. He sold it originally when one of his oil company stocks struck a gusher. He was back in town soon later with the news the gusher had done gone dry and he was left with worthless stock. Old, old man Trainor owned it for a while and it eventually ended up in the hands of Hub Zeches who sold it to Art Cunningham. It's a good place to hear the stories the dead have to tell. Soon as I sat down, one of them sat beside me and started talking.

"Art Cunningham made me the man I was. Art knew how to deal with us boys whose wiring wasn't normal. His cast of characters that he employed were life lessons walking. I can't tell you how many bowls of oyster stew I had sitting at the counter listening to

Jeannie and Sophie talking yesterday. Sophie, she used to check the milk temperature of my oyster stew with her finger before serving at the counter with the Marigold milk sign on the back wall. Too hot a soup leaves a bad taste in your mouth, I recall her saying. People who just didn't fit into the hole felt at home in the Hurry Back you see. Rubbing shoulders with us townies made you a better person to my way of thinking. And if you fit in all too well in the real world, well your seeing would soon change for the better. I mean seeing Chinky Deerman shining shoes was a memory that's gets etched into a man's thinking.

"Once I stepped into the Hurry Back I could feel myself breathing. My mind left the dead zone that school brought and I felt normal, alive inside the four walls of the Hurry Back. I was a Hurry Back boy and carried it to my grave."

"Can I ask your name?" I asked.

"Jim, but my name don't matter. Art Cunningham gave me a chance. He showed me a way. And for every Jim, there's a Bob or a Frank or a Steve that can tell you a story.

"Art Cunningham cared for everybody. He didn't care which side of the tracks you came from. I don't think I ever met a man more comfortable with the clothes he was wearing. Art got me a job with the Railroad. Railroad life isn't for everyone but Art told me to never quit. I retired as a railman and when I hear the name Cunningham I stop in my tracks, take a deep breath, think about what might have been and thank Art."

##

My knees were aching. My joints were pounding. I looked at the clock. It was 3 AM. Dead people talking.

I headed downstairs. My head was spinning. Went to the garage and started my car. Drove off searching for the dead folk.

I could hear the sounds of the East End calling. I parked in front of Robb Brothers Hardware. I took in a deep breath taking in the beautiful night sky hovering over Winona town.

"Hanson, come sit," I heard coming from the stoop of the small church at 4th and Carimona. I have a hard time seeing what with cataracts floating all over my vision. 'Bout all I could make out was a white throat, glasses, and the burning tip of a cigar. I moved slowly sitting down on the stoop next to him.

"Here, have a sip," he said handing me the bottle. "I know I shouldn't drink. Days like this. You won't be telling Bishop Cotter, will you? He ships us drinking priests out of town. It brings me clarity and an easing of the pain that the Polish immigrants endured. I heard their stories, seen their actions, and sometimes you just want to cry."

"Mighty tasty," I said, taking a swig.

"Joe Milanowski gets it for me. Lives right over at 557 East Second. A crafty politician cutting deals on both sides. Right from the still of Jacob and Alex Pellofski, he tells me. The best around. Why they even ship their product to Chicago. Joe sends my whiskey over in a cigar box. Those Nuns keep an eye on me you know, and they'll tolerate a cigar as long as I don't light it in the Sacristy. All business, those Notre Dame nuns are and they, like Cotter, don't take much to drinking. What brings you down here?"

"Sore knees. We had an agreement. You dead folk agreed not to wake me. At your beckoning call anytime, but you are not to interrupt my sleep."

"It wasn't something I attended. It's the power of the spirit which brought us together. You should have been here when they tore this church down and built that big red monstrosity. We held mass in the basement of St. Johns over on Sixth. Those old Polish ladies didn't much care for that Bohemian God. Ask any Polish person and they'll tell you the only pure God is the Polish one.

"A Whiskey and a cigar. One of life's pleasures, taking me away from the burdens of living. I woke just after midnight. Another child dead. 14 years old. A Czaplewski girl. She had been assaulted just two days prior to her dying. I had married her parents and baptized her. She was a beautiful young girl in her first communion dress. Boys who did it will get off scot-free. One of the reasons I drink."

I sat on that stoop just staring at that night sky wondering what kind of God would allow this. What would cause a man or men to do such a horrific act? I took a sip of my whiskey and lit up my own cigar as life spoke. I never did get the priest's name. He sure could pound whiskey, and I can't say I blame him.

##

"I tell you, Hanson, I'll never forget my first trip thru the Hurry Back. I was just a little kid. Must have been 4 or 5. Grandpa brought me down here. It was Christmas eve morning and he picked me up early, winking at Ma saying we got some business to take care of downtown. Ma got a worried look in her eye knowing Grandpa and business usually meant a phone call from some bar near closing time. Grandpa liked to drink.

"He told me we were going to have ourselves a great time. Christmas Eve morning the whole town is out. Drinking coffee, buying last minute gifts. Laughing and carrying on. People are always happier when they are spending money, buying something for others. It's a magical time seeing the spirit that rests in us.

"Of course, I was just a little tyke, wide eyed and believing whatever my Grandpa told me. He really liked telling stories and though he only lived another year or so I think it was his storytelling that made me fall in love with Winona.

"We started that day at the Kewpee Café. He bought me a piece of rhubarb pie. Ma was never much for baking, so this rhubarb pie was a real treat. I noticed he carried a small little metal bottle with a screw top that he poured into his coffee. When I asked him, he said it was just a little fuel for his coffee. Get his insides right.

"We were just starting our day so as I finished my pie and Grandpa finished his second cup of coffee out the door we headed saying goodbye to Auntie Francis. Kitty Corner we went, stopping at Ruth's Restaurant. I remember feeling tension showing in my Grandpa's demeanor, but he was determined to tell me about all the folks of Winona. He was a Kewpee man. I think it was the red booths that made him nervous. I've never felt real comfortable wearing or driving red. I like to blend in, observe, not be seen. Anyway, family trait."

The guy kept talking. I took a look around at my surroundings. I was sitting in the back of the Hurry Back. The Post office towered over the block. Smith's Winona Furniture was near across the way. It was and is a narrow alley. Probably just wide enough for an Anderson Rubbish truck to get thru, maybe. Horses I'm sure back in the day. One of Winona's talking alleys when we didn't have parking lots. Memories got a way of echoing. I had another hit off my smoke and paid him attention.

"He had another two cups of coffee and a pour in each. I had French Fries. We finished and left saying goodbye to Darlene and Ruth, walked by the Dairy Bar, thinking we were heading in and I asked. He shuddered and said the words don't match. Sometimes he spoke in riddles that no four year old was going to understand. I was just ecstatic I tell you.

"We stopped in at Neville's and Grandpa squirmed as he sat. We had coffee and pop at Kresge's and Woolworth's. He pointed to the Morgan Block and said that it was the heart and soul of this town except for the Hurry Back. Some of his favorite places. It wasn't until years later after he was gone that I realized Grandpa had a hard time staying out of bars and it was equally difficult for him to leave them once he was in them. The Morgan Block held some of his favorite haunts.

"To the Hurry Back we went and then out the front door of Kresge's. It's a shame you know. It was the coolest looking building downtown. Hurry Back Billiards. It said hello before you ever walked inside. Welcome. We'll take your downtrodden and poor, your misguided, your misdirected. It spoke not only Winona but America to my way of understanding. Made you feel right at home. I mean I was young and I saw Sophie dip her finger in Grandpa's stew. I met Chinky and I heard Grandpa's whisper that's fear you're feeling. He's a good person to steer clear of unless you need your shoes shined. Best in the country he said. Ben Lee sat in his Barber's chair reading the paper. Grandpa didn't bring me into the pool hall where it was said you could cut the smoke with a knife. That's when I looked to my left.

"Sitting four seats down from me was Santa Claus himself. Mr. Cunningham was serving him eggs and pie and milkshakes, malts. Anything he wanted.

I remember Art saying, 'It's a big night for you Santa. Gotta, fill your tummy. And here' some Zagnut candy bars for the reindeer.'

"Of all the places to stop Santa chose The Hurry Back. My greatest Christmas ever. Full believing. He could have stopped anywhere. The place was magic, Hanson."

Rambles

It was one of those perfect Minnesota evenings. A little breezy and the water was running fast, just a bit high, keeping those skeeters and gnats from doing their thing but the sun felt nice and warmed the remnants of winter still in me.

We were sitting on the deck of the railroad machine shop, staring out at the Wisconsin bluffs and Levee Park. In the old days we'd seen the Mississippi River flowing, but flooding took away the old Levee.

Science girl was with me trying to keep me upright. She was a master at that and her keeping me wobbling was part of our dance. Soon as my mind started drifting away from the beauty of the land and moment, she'd change the radio station running through my head and then laugh as I got back in focus.

When I tried explaining how the dead were talking, she started talking about energy fields and molecules and the speed of light. I took a sip of the Mexican Mule and prepared to hear about the formation of the stone upon which we walk when she said she was sensing her past. Something, rumbling deep inside her.

Being a townie and not very good at science I had decided to take a jab at her science thinking, asking her, "Could you put a measurement on those feelings. Numbers? You have to have some data to make your claim," I said.

"I know what I feel! You trying to tell me what I'm feeling? Do my feelings not exist in your solid state? Those feelings tell me I once roamed this earth a long time ago in a bloody French Pub. I ran a brothel!" Her eyes blazed and I knew I had overstepped my bounds, telling a woman what she was feeling was a short trip to hell, and I was getting too old to sleep outside. She looked at me, through her magnifying lenses. Her beautiful eyes had a way of dancing, bouncing, jumpy, nuggets of living inside the lights of her pupils. She can light up a room with just her being.

But on this beautiful evening those beautiful eyes had turned stormy. Dead dog serious, she said, "Science is coming ever closer to understanding human nature. Serotonin is lacking in the children of misfortune. Epigenetics."

I shook my head saying, "Serotonin?"

"Yes," she said. "A chemical produced by your brain, your thinking. It provides calm to your being. A pause between thoughts before reacting."

I didn't ask her all the XY gene stuff, and I'm guessing we've started reaching a greater understanding of the genetic code. Science has the best chance to fix us when we push our fears away.

"A little Serotonin don't hurt nobody, all of us need a little calming to the engine in us. A life without calm, peace can't be satisfying."

I hear the mills of Bay State talking quietly as they turn brown grains into green money inside the machinations of modern industry. The boys get shorter who carry the bags of flour that turn to bread, and Science girl was saying how severe trauma is being passed on to the next generation through genetic mutation.

"Like a science fiction novel?" I asked.

She nodded, and I heard a voice just over my left ear. "Poor girl understands your thinking Hanson. Poor girl, having to figure out what kind of baggage you are carrying in your thinking."

"It's nice not being alone," I chuckled.

Science Girl glared. "Talking to the dead? There ain't nothing there."

I stared out onto the park. Birds were chirping and the air cooled my senses.

The guy kept whispering. "I was an old railman. 40 years. This is where I worked before it became a restaurant. Name of Jick. It was Art Cunningham who taught me life. School wasn't for me. I started working at the Hurry Back. Didn't have no direction. I worked at the Hurry Back doing anything Art wanted. Art was a good man. He worked nights for the railroad. Worked the tower, nights. Rails never rest. He got me the job at the railroad. Never quit he said. I had a good life. Wouldn't have been possible without Art."

Science Girl was carrying on at the same time. "We aren't in the business of repeat after me. Tomorrow, tomorrow can be such a better place. Science a pursuit of a better way, a greater understanding." It was Cheryl keeping my one foot in the sane lane. My science thinking doesn't go deep enough but then again Science Girl didn't always hear the dead. Proof that love don't always work out as planned.

"Do you see the mounds?" a new voice whispered. "Straight ahead. My burial spot. Not a nicer place in the world to spend your dying days and I can't imagine a finer place to be as I worked my way through my passages of time. My eternity. I felt the warmth of Mother Earth all around me," he whispered. "I loved this river and the birds and the hawks and eagles and the fish. It provided us with food and a story to live proudly by. A shame my mound is no more.

"Today your world moves so fast. Hurrying, hurrying to get somewhere else only finding you'd rather be in a different place. No wonder you don't get along with those who think different. Listen, listen to the river and ask yourself what it is saying as it goes past us. My name was River Talk and the river has always had a way of talking when you cared to listen."

Science Girl looked at me and downed her drink. A fine Minnesota evening just watching time pass as yesterday started speaking.

The evening faded from my seeing, and a new voice took my attention. "This is Stoner out driving the roads of America. Here we are testing out the people's van, me and Cindi. It's got all the features a person can want. We don't drive too fast anymore. We prefer the slow lane, listening to our own kind of music, hearing our own yesterday so we might only travel a couple hundred miles a day when we are road tripping, space cruising and so we charge it when we stop."

Stoner's voice crackled over the radio in my head. "Me and Cindi like the unusual. Preferring to drive the back roads, eat breakfast at roadside diners and find a campground where we seem to fall asleep shortly after raising our spirits to the gods of the night sky. I find myself once a month when that full moon rises, finding the perfect spot for camping all mapped and charted for optimal light. I watch that weather making sure we get a clear night where the full moon illuminates the night sky. Cindi just isn't right when she can't dance under the full moon. Something builds up inside her, raising her internal thermostat. That's when she explodes and I'm getting too old to see unhappiness. Dancing under the full moon helps Cyndy. We've been together a long time now and so we know the patterns of each other. I smile as she starts taking off her white bathrobe with the big red rose on it and she puts on her tie dye skirts, shirts and scarfs. That full moon dances with the spirit resting in her. I can hear her breathing. I can smell her smell. I see her bopping, dancing under that night sky. Moonbeams reflecting the slow love oozing through me. Dancing, slow dancing."

Another voice interrupted him. "Stoner, Stoner we cannot have this sensual, intimate talk on the radio. Mr. J will have a bird, offending his sensibilities like you do, much less the FCC. They are all over us trying to figure out where are feed is transmitted from. And now you're talking about a seductive dance?" It was Braveheart down at the radio station. She'd been hearing and seeing the dead down on Third Street from the days of the Club Bar and Nasty Habit. Poor girl had opened a whole new world in her thinking when she took some of that purple microdot in the 70's. It was her vision and Timothy McMood. A genius that detected energy coming from tombstones. Don't ask me how.

Stoner answered in a voice full of melancholy. "The hardest thing about being dead, Braveheart. You can't touch. Gone once that casket closes. So I got this beautiful women dancing, slow, seductive, dancing right in front of me and I can't do a thing about it. I feel young and alive again but without touch you feel the pain of being alone."

Braveheart was now running the radio station. Corporate buy out, some big-time communications company out of a PO Box in the Virgin Islands was now the owner. One of their wonks up in the corporate chain must have detected a changing in a market, listening demands and found this little bitty radio station to have all the growth signs that made the cash register ring. They bought the station from Mr. J who was hopelessly attached to another era and was now the face for the absentee owners.

I was thinking about Stoner, and Science Girl was still carrying on about the genetic mutations being induced from trauma, when I heard more voices coming from the woodwork.

A stern voice broke in, blocking out Stoner and Science Girl both. "They got numbers, satellite monitoring of your doings, Hanson. Numbers on everything. An algorithm. A pattern, data derived. Everything is collected, analyzed, and processed. Bosses looking at the standards line for deviations that become trends. A number is all that we've become."

"Professor Jarvinen, I'm being what? I'm being monitored, watched?"

I'm listening to Stoner on the radio, nodding my head to Science Girl, and now an old mathematics professor is speaking to me from the brick walls of the old railroad building that became a restaurant.

"Yes, your footprints, the traces of where you were, digitalized patterns. Machines, applying that data. Freedom? You are just a pawn, a speckle of star dust. A number. The god myth is faltering as those machines gather data and pulses of energy. Control, it is all about control. Lights and color, the visuals, driving us.

"Privacy, a faded memory of yesterday," he said "Silent monitoring of all you do. Cameras, satellites everywhere, uploading your digital footprint. Just another number is what we've become. Faceless entities going through life wishing they were somewhere else."

Science Girl clapped her hand on my knee. "You didn't hear a thing I said, did you? You know what it's like? A partner who doesn't listen. Who has his mind elsewhere," Science Girl said. "It didn't register in your thinking that those who undergo trauma, pass that lack of feeling onto the next generation? Nothing the kids can do; it is in the genes. The children of trauma got no serotonin in their being, and you wonder why things are getting worse."

I nodded as I took a slow sip of that Mexican Mule and waited for the next rant.

##

I took a glance at the filled chairs of the Vivian Fusillo Theatre on the Winona State University Campus. It was opening night of the Great River Shakespeare Festival and most everyone was engrossed in the story of MacBeth. My mind drifted.

"Death is no place to be carrying the sins of your living." Stoner sat beside me. "You think the game ends when the light turns dark. You know so little about the journey everyone goes through. Death might wake you up." He was whispering in my ear that the words start making sense when you catch the rhythm of the character and don't worry about the meaning of every word. "Shakespeare has a way of understanding human nature and the frailties of the human psyche," Stoner said. "Mr. William, he has a way of speaking the truth in his works."

I looked around and saw Newspaper man, Paint man, Coke man and Banker man. If they were hearing Stoner, they were paying him no attention. Science Girl and friends, Christine and Fred, were focused on the play in front of them not hearing the whispers that I did. Those sins of greed and lust and envy like the devil himself entered the thinking of Macbeth played superbly by Andrew Carlson.

"Poor man didn't stand a chance," Stoner whispered. "She is evil," he added as Lady Macbeth planted seeds in Macbeth's thinking. "The Devil's helper she is."

Leah Gabriel, Lady MacBeth, played the slow descent into the world of insanity well, literally cracking right in front of our eyes. Killing must weigh heavy on the mind of those who engage in the act or at least it used to.

I heard Stoner gasp when Macbeth hopped up on top of the dining room table, and newspaper man pointed out to me as we got a beverage during intermission that the sword fights were done superbly. I told him the lighting, the set, and the sounds brought the audience closer into the soul of Macbeth.

Stoner stayed with me. "Don't let anybody fool you," he said. "We all got a bit of Macbeth in us. Tortured souls lusting for power. MacBeth, you blood thirsty bastard," Stoner screamed. "The stains of your sins remain long after you leave life and enter the darkness. Wash, wash the hands of your evil but there is no escaping that darkness which will soon fall upon your head."

When the play was over, we drifted to the bench that Christine's family had purchased for the campus. I sat and slowly let the Surly IPA release the bonds that tie you to a well-directed play. Phelps school loomed in front of me, and the darkened playground I had scraped my knee upon and the slide I cut open my head upon were now just a distant memory. I wondered where Stoner had gone.

Christine, Fred, and Science Girl thought the performance was superbly directed by Paul Barnes and that the Vivian Fusillo Theatre was worthy of such a fine performance. A fine Saturday night with friends.

As we were walking back to the car my phone rang. It was Stoner again, and I asked him where he had gone.

He said, "I stopped in and saw Big D at his house over by the power plant. The light was on you know?"

"A new shipment?" I asked.

He chuckled, coughed, and whispered, "Columbian. All is right with me. Got no worries. Later, Gator."

I felt myself warming. It brought me pleasure hearing a calm, contented Stoner. That war had twisted his brain and if any man should have pleasure Stoner was it.

Stoner's internal wiring went from relaxed to fast so you had to enjoy the calm while you could. Never lasted long. It was near the fourth of July and with all the flags on display and the sounds of war, fireworks, echoing off the buildings Stoner was more than likely to lose it.

Stoner didn't much like war. He went to Nam because that's what Stoner Thompson and his family did. The Thompson men served this country, going back to the Revolution. Some nights Stoner would get talking about how war changed his life and the whiskey bottle was close.

Stoner was a mess, so you needed to move slow as he told the story of the demons that never left him. He saw things at a young age, that no man, women, child, should ever have to see. He told me how the blown-up body of his buddy, Jimmy, splattered on his uniform.

"The taste of death never leaves," he raised his voice. "Right there, right there, living one minute, gone the next. Not a body left to bury. Blood splattered, skin clinging to the trees, bones scattered and splintered. Jimmy Boylan, dead in the jungles of Nam. To Captain Boylan," he roared as he raised his glass and threw it at the brick wall just behind Walt Newman's place. To the good Jimmy Boylan," and he started singing. "Oh, Jimmy Boy, Jimmy Boy, the pipes are calling."

I knew my time was ending with Stoner as that whiskey twisted his thinking, turning him a deep shade of dark and those demons circled in every direction. He'd be drinking with dead buddies as he retreated into that world where only those who've walked the dark alleys and places where hope is gone would understand.

Stoner kept talking. "We gathered what was left of Jimmy, placed him on a stretcher, said a prayer for his soul and walked him back to camp amidst the sounds of the jungle in a foreign land. Back to camp where we said a last goodbye as we put the remnants of Jimmy's living in a body bag."

Stoner stared at me and unleashed every four-letter word I knew letting me know it was time for me to leave. "Why are we fighting?" he screamed. "Suits sent us boys to die while their kids went off to make their fortune."

Fred, Christine and Science Girl were carrying on with their own reality. I turned to Fred saying, "July 4th in 1863 was one of Stoner's most worrisome days. Celebrating the death of seven thousand men. On the souls of men whose life ended too soon, they made a national holiday. Gettysburg where 7000 died and the brave Minnesota boys turned Robert E Lee around. Dead they lay. Unburied on the fields of Gettysburg as the town folk tried put the pieces back together. Old ladies and kids hardly big enough to turn a shovel buried the bloated bodies of man and horse alike. Old men, too old to serve, did what they could. Flies feasting on the dead and the fresh vomit from the gravediggers. The stench of death and decay whistled through and around the town that saw the turning tide of war as Lee headed south cut off by the valiant Minnesota boys and their suicide charge. Right there at Cemetery Ridge, life lost. Nearly seven thousand dead in a battle of grit and courage."

Science Girl cackled, "Let's get him home. Dead people start going through his thinking and who knows what he'll say next."

Fred started the car.

Christine said, "Let's hear some John Lennon."

Science Girl played Imagine as we rolled down the windows and a beautiful Winona night filled our senses, blocking for a moment, those images of death and destruction.

A week later, my eyes were watering. Full to the brim. I had just witnessed an amazing one actor play called No Child at the Vivian Fusillo Theatre on the Winona State Campus.

I had picked up old friend Carol as Cheryl was out celebrating her birthday in Boston and Maine with lifelong friends. She had made arrangements, so I would remain a bit sane from her leaving me in charge of my own vices.

Carol had grown up in the neighborhood. One of those big, beautiful houses that is now a memory. The Miller Brothers Engineering building now stands where once a family lived with a half dozen yipping and yapping Pomeranians.

Before the show, we walked past the house where music teacher, Carlis Anderson had lived. Miss Anderson went on Sabbatical one year and us Goodview boys who mostly couldn't sing, dance, or play an instrument, twisted that substitute teacher in the wind.

Carol reminisced about mooning people out that oval shaped window on the second floor of the Durfey Home. She giggled, and I wondered if kids still mooned and laughed.

We continued our walk admiring old houses, the architecture and the dead people who once slept in those homes. That whole block is filled with older homes just wanting to talk. I saw young Burmie, running, and I wondered where he was headed.

At the end of the block, across the street in the Congo parking lot, an old tree stood on the corner, gnarled and twisted like a tree rooted in rock. It once had a full head of leaves and before it lost its hair it stood proud as if running against life itself. I remembered standing on the corner admiring its tortured beauty near five years back when a wise, wise lady of the grey house stepped out and told me the tree's name and origin. Forgetting seems to happen more often every day as life and its beat just seems faster.

We walked toward campus and grade school and talked of our early teachers and friends we hadn't seen lately. Taught by grey haired ladies who never married, we learned to read and write and think. That black iron fence which used to enclose the school more than likely ended up at Millers junkyard where it got crushed, broken down, and reused in a different form.

We talked of old libraries and alleys we used to walk and run through on our way to nowhere. That pathway between Somson and Phelps, just past the Magnolia Tree which blooms fine fragrance every spring, shook my senses as I remembered my early days of learning. We remembered Mr. Brooks and Mr. Theis, and Carol reflected warmly on Miss Bucher who once taught at the school and outfitted the Phelps cheerleaders.

We headed over to the theatre and were entertained by The Riverland Jazz Festival which played in the center of campus. Beautiful horns and saxes played soft and the breeze quietly carried the music to the campuses far reaches. It was a beautiful day and I found myself drifting to the music as Carol munched on a hamburger and we waited for the show to open.

Carol finished her hamburger, and we went inside. I was a bit baffled as I entered the smaller performance theatre. A metal detector stood right in the way and when the beep went off shortly after I walked through, I heard Stoner whisper sorry and realized I'm never alone. Stoner forgot he was carrying a pipe.

I heard Stoner whisper, "They can't see me, but that pipe I carried from my living days sets things off."

I just shook my head and thought of younger days. We sat along the back wall, and I felt safe not having to worry about those demons getting me from behind.

I asked Stoner what he thought of the play and he said, "The less you know the better. All you need to know is she don't talk like Shakespeare. I never saw anybody act like Mellisa Maxwell. She plays like 12 different characters without missing a beat. An amazing face that turned and stretched in every direction as she played every one of those characters. She can flat out act. Director Tarah Flanagan and Miss Maxwell pulled off a Masterpiece."

I looked at Carol whose eyes were intent on the stage as the play opened. The rumbling worked its way through the audience as the stage slowly dimmed, and Carol was focused on the play. She didn't hear or see Stoner.

For a little over an hour Ms. Maxwell worked the stage as she played a dead janitor and students, a principle, a teacher, and talked with parents. She did it without a hiccup, a break or even a misplaced line and by the end of the play my eyes were filled with water. I remembered how fortunate I was in attending Winona schools and how the changes we've seen come over our lives these past four decades have taken root in perhaps our most important responsibility.

We met Miss Maxwell as we left the theatre, warm, gracious and kind. I was amazed after such a brilliant performance there was no edge, no unwinding to her demeanor. A remarkable performance.

Carol and I headed to McVeys, now called Mugby Junction. Light music played overhead, and we unwound from a wonderful evening. Thank you, Shakespeare and company.

##

It was quiet in the car as Science Girl and I headed out for the North Shore. It was our chance, to recharge, rejuvenate and relax. We could feel the sounds of yesterday's narrative leaving us as we headed North to the big lake.

We were hoping to leave all the dead folks back in Winona. Recharge our batteries. The dead, it seems, don't take no for an answer, and it wasn't more than a few minutes before I heard them talking, whispering as we drove up the Wisconsin way.

That scratchy, raspy voice coming out of the back seat was Emil Nigorski. He said the boys down at the Legion had given him a bit of money to go visit his friend Zeke up in Two Harbors. Zeke sold the finest mushrooms and his mushroom pizza made him forget all that ails him.

Now Emil was not quite right in the head, and it wasn't because of the war. His thinking has always been a nickel short and three days late. He served and served well. Everybody loved Emil. A shame he couldn't hold down work. No matter how many times you told him he wouldn't remember.

He leaned on the back of the seat and scratched out his words. "I feel comfortable around men who served. I was a soldier, a good soldier," he said. "Hut, two, three. Attention. But I couldn't handle Korea. It was a different place. A tension in the air. Made me nervous. All wound up on my insides. I'd a snapped had I had to stay in those lands much longer. You've entered the land of shadows and they talk. Life in a different light.

"They thought I was weak and not worthy was what they whispered. Nothing wrong with him they say. Looks just like you and me. Weak I tell yah, couldn't face dying he heard coming from old warriors. I heard them," he snarled, "Whispers every which way I went."

"Wild Zeke's Pizza Cafe fixes what ails me, just down from the National Tea Grocery Store on the main drag of Two Harbors, Minnesota. Zeke, you see uses the real mushrooms he finds foraging in the woods for his pies. So good, so good it changes my thinking. Blood pressure, tension gone. I tell yah when I was living I could head up here to the North Shore and have one of Zeke's pizzas and all the angers, anxiety, worries that followed this veteran of the Korean War gone. When are you coming back from your excursion up North?" he asked.

"Sunday," I said loudly, and Science Girl stopped talking. She'd been talking about dominant species and their time in Geologic terms.

"Who are we traveling with?" she asked.

I whispered, "Nigorski."

She asked about his sweet soul and I told her that the demons seem to be sleeping inside him.

"Don't be the fuel," I said to her.

She paused, took a deep breath and said, "This is perfect weather, a crispness in the air and people got bounces in their steps. We got ourselves some chilling, relaxing in front of us and I don't want him interrupting your thinking. He ain't staying with us, is he?"

"No, no I said we have to drop him off at his buddy's place in downtown Two Harbors."

"Zeke's Wild Mushroom Pizza?" she asked.

"Yeah, how'd you know?" I said.

"Frank used to talk about it all the time back when he was living. Zeke though, has got to be dead. I met him once back in the 80's and he must have been near 90 then."

"You can't ever leave Indian land," came the scratchy voice from the back seat. "They were tied to nature, the people of the lands. Way back to the Ojibwa. Life as told in the waters of the Gitche Gummie. Wild Zeke understood that spirit that sits in the heart of man," Emil said, half interrupting Science Girl who kept right on talking.

I looked at Science Girl and my heart flittered. I don't think she was yet hearing the dead folk, but she was getting mighty good at sensing them. Emil said he'd let us find our own spirit while he recaptured his at Zeke's.

"Is that it?" she asked.

"I don't think so," I replied. I smelled the burnt tobacco, Half n Half. "I think Dad hitched a ride. He doesn't talk much anymore you know. Getting out and about, seeing what he missed is what he is today. Lotta catching up in walking those State Parks now that walking isn't as hard as when he was living."

"You are a messed-up guy," Science Girl said as she smiled.

"Like a new day every day," I replied.

"Let's stop at Kendall's Fish Market just outside of Two Harbors on the National Scenic Byway before dropping Emil off. Just up here on the left."

I could feel the vacation starting.

We found a place to stay at the Cove Lodge just outside of Beaver Bay, Minnesota, population 181. It's a nice place. Our room was on the second floor with 3 big windows which we kept open to hear the waves of the big lake. Fireplace and jacuzzi too. Science Girl likes nice things even though she's a rock climbing, dirt digging small town girl at heart. Her brain can get a bit scrambled, moves too fast and she can't hardly see, but she's a keeper.

I started talking to Mickey as Science Girl was still living in the world of dreams and unknowns. It was his fish house on the edge of the Cove property.

He waved me over for a cup of coffee and a smoke, just about the time the sun was rising. Morning at the Cove Lodge and Resort. "You come up here. Hanson, thinking you know most everything living along that Mississippi River. This here big lake will put you in your place. If it doesn't rumble through you, if it don't churn your heart, you got no soul, no gumption. Go ahead sit here on the porch, walk the rocks and soon you'll realize how much better you can be. No place I would have rather lived than right here along the North Shore. The greatest lake of them all right outside my door.

"We buried Mama in the bottom of that lake," he carried on. "Like she wanted. It was a lake of the spirits she used to say. She wanted to spend that next life with the spirits that lay deep down in that lake. The great below she used to say. I can hear her yet today. 'You hear their voices, Pa? Mickey can you hear them?' She'd be just a staring and her arms would be flailing, back and forth, pacing, moving. 'Grandpa, Grandpa, oh good seeing you. I so miss your laugh.' She would carry on a conversation all night, talking to people none of us could see. 'Can't you see them, Pa?'

"Pa swore me to silence, saying if I said a thing about her talking with the dead to anyone she'd get sent to the asylum. Those people don't come back. Forever forgotten.

"She would carry on for hours until Pa brought out his fiddle. It had a way of reaching her and in no time at all Pa would have her dancing. Slow at first, working that music, working inside her. Pretty soon Pa would get to playing that Orange Blossom Special and her feet and hands and legs were moving in every which direction, faster and faster till she'd sit down laughing, no longer able to keep up. Every night before they went to bed, he'd play Amazing Grace in honor of those who'd left before her. Summers, falls and early winter were happy, happy times.

"I must have been seven or so when she started falling apart.

Those early spring months. The old folk called it cabin fever, and it ran strong in her. She just wasn't right in the head. She'd start talking all the time to things we couldn't see. Singing old spirituals and whaling like death lay on her doorstep.

"The family had come here early in the settling of these parts. Like the Ojibwa before us the lake gave us a sense of place. A sense of identity. Mostly we liked the isolation and being part of and surrounded by nature. It's pretty and peaceful up here in the winter when the winter winds ain't beating you down. Sometimes that sun shines and the great lake gets still. Cutting and stacking wood under a beautiful February sun, in my long johns is as good as it gets. You living folk live in that noisy world you've created. Can't be good for any sense of peace.

"Mama she wasn't right in the head, but she had a place in my soul that never left. She had always insisted she be buried at Sea. Join the great spirits of the lake she would cry. Pa and I of course didn't say a thing. No use arguing when she was having one of her spells.

"It was sad, the day she passed. Right there on that rocking chair that you are sitting on. We carried her out to where we had the boat tied up. Pa had an old Johnson Outboard with not a lot of juice, and we'd crafted together a stretcher out of the branches and limbs of the forest. She said she wanted to go to the other side just wearing her everyday clothes. Her comfortable clothes. So me and Pa filled her pockets with stones, tying her down with heavy rocks and Pa drove that little boat with the 3hp engine as far out to the middle of the lake as one could see.

"Ma had requested we play Orange Blossom Special before we said our final goodbye. She'd winked and had said it was to be sure that she really was dead. Give her a jolt of energy for the next leg she said. Pa fiddled the song that moved her out there on the big lake as we remembered her. That smile and laugh that always came after the playing. Pa nodded to me, and we gently placed her in the cold, cold waters of Lake Superior. We watched, as her body slowly dropped into deeper waters. Pops, he could make that fiddle sing and as we sat out there on the patch of water where Mama got buried, we remembered her light that she brought to our being."

##

It was only a matter of time. Drones, small little drones carrying a miniaturized load of explosives falling from the sky. It didn't hit us today, but the day is coming, sure as shooting. Technology trickles down.

We've made a lot of enemies during these many years of constant fighting. Been fighting since Korea and killing another is sure to make enemies as brothers rise to avenge the death of their brothers. Bombs with 'Made in the USA' being the business card left behind in our enemy's land. Seeds of anger, and we say deal with it.

Like in the playgrounds of our youth, eventually that skinny, scrawny kid wearing glasses will exact his revenge as he punches the bully in the mouth with all the anger of being oppressed. Been happening for years in our schools, and it seems our foreign military policies are all about power and bigger guns. Drones are small, the miniaturization of electronic components ever more deadly.

We've been dropping bombs on the heads of countries since forever. We've bombed other country's people, innocents and their buildings that had meaning to them. What has all the fighting brought us? A safer world?

We know full well American terrorists roam this land and sooner rather than later whether it be a foreigner or a born in the USA terrorist, it will happen. Drones can be bought, and men driven by hate can program them to strike the targets of their anger. It can happen in America and those drones listen to people of all ethnicities, all colors, all religions.

Peace and love those old pot smoking, acid dropping hippies used to say. Maybe, just maybe they were right.

##

I was sitting in Broken World Records sharing an Absinthe with Science girl. She was carrying on about her day while I was feeling and seeing the shadows circling.

Absinthe was the drink of choice for the painters like Vincent Van Gogh and Paul Gauguin in the 1880's. A den of artists and painters and thinkers and writers all living in Paris and drinking and talking at cafes. Late rising mornings. It tastes a bit like black licorice, but it isn't the taste, but the way it talks to a person that makes it interesting.

The Minnesota Maritime Art Museum, right out there on the road heading to Prairie Island have a couple of their works hanging on the walls and if you look at the early work of Van Gogh and his later works something happened to his thinking as color and light entered his picture making.

At one time, Broken World Records was the American Legion Bar and before that it was the Lincoln Hotel. In its early days there was a second floor where people slept and stayed. It was packed here in 2020 with the faces of yesterday showing up in their windows of time.

I could feel the tension as we made our way into the bar. Men of war waiting for a call. The men were gloomy wondering how to fight a war against something they couldn't see. The gun was no solution.

"This is beyond the shadows," old soldier Olson was saying from across the way. The vets from WW1, Ben and Harry, just shook their heads and quietly drank having faced the flu near the end of that first war. Shell shocked boys in a bar full of soldiers and their wives who were once dames now bearing the scars and wrinkles that come from living and dying.

Science Girl was talking about stars exploding and imploding and how the ages of history are shown in the rocks. "Footprints left behind as the signs of life happened," she said. "Late to the dance we were."

"I'm not dancing, and my bones have the stiffness starting to settle."

She struck me across the shoulder and said, "That isn't what I meant."

The old folks murmured that this war would end the lives of their closest links to their past. No greater pain then seeing a person die before their time, seeing someone pass. Children in another's eye and the old folks dying were the children to a bygone yesterday.

The folks at the bar worried. We were under attack from

something we couldn't see, and our guns can't kill what they can't see. People, dropping dead all over the world and the folks sitting round that bar didn't like the feeling of helplessness. "The worst thing," old lady Singer said. "These bugs must be atheists, being it seems all the praying in the world couldn't stop them.

One guy slid up right next to me, shoulder to shoulder saying social distancing isn't necessary for us dead folks. "We have immunity, Hanson. My name is General Mags. I worked in Military intelligence. When I first started, I did it the old-fashioned way. I listened on street corners and bars and would spend time at an old bird feeder on park benches watching Military Brass coming and going. Every night I would write reports about what I saw and heard. My German was good having been educated in the Winona schools and St. Martins where old folks still talked German. Lots of Taufel, in my upbringing, that's the devil in German. Tell your readers it's pronounced 'toy full'," he said.

I asked, "How'd you get your information out of Germany?"

He said, "I don't know beyond the drop. Somethings you just don't want to know. Fraulein Helga was my drop. We played the game of romance for all to see." His eyes rolled back to another time and said, "She was a large, large women who talked like a man and barked orders. She was the cook for the Comandant Kreutschwitz, and I gave her the spy notes that she passed to the next link.

"Her father had been part of the Weimar Republic, a slightly above middling bureaucrat. Helga loved her Daddy who was a wide, large man. We would spend evenings together, displaying feigned romance when seen. Helga would cook for me and tell me stories of her family and of the Germany she knew and loved.

"When she told me that Hitler had executed her father for acts betraying the German identity, I understood why she did what she did. A great spy for the American cause, and she never left her Germany. We would talk all night, and her reflections on her Germanic myth were woven into the stories I told of what was happening in Germany during that Second war.

"Where those notes went, I am not sure," he said. "I could tell as time passed, they were being read as the tides of war began turning. Watching for the unusual patterns as a rhythm started taking over a country and it's being. Helga marched and talked the Nazi way all the while she revealed and passed on secrets under the eye of the bastard Commandant."

Science girl nudged me and said she wanted another Absinthe. "Make sure it's got the wormwood and thank Commander Mags for his service," she said.

##

Me and Science Girl were out walking our way through the refuge when I heard the whispering. Dead people, dead people out and about, all around the paths. They were all smiling, beaming on a beautiful day. Listen to the trees, the leaves, the river, the birds and the ducks.

I hear them whispering. Nature will tell you a story of life, death, and rebirth. It's the cycle of life, and you'll find more meaning to the world you left when you spend a day in the Mississippi Wildlife Refuge.

A voice grew clearer through the whispers. "Nature, nature I had it in me from my youngest days. Dad, he was a Game Warden who did his job well. He carried with him a love of the outdoors and on Saturday mornings him and I would head outside. We'd buy a Bloedow's and head across the river. He called it the old country where distant relatives still lived. We would fish and help our old family with the odds and ends that come from living. I went to Cotter and St. Mary's. Married and had five wonderful children. It's a bit nicer with Mom joining me.

"It has been a long time since I've seen nature so happy and healthy. Nature rebounding, changing and the clean air filling the sky. I do worry about the trees. All this rain the past few years. Taking the roots. Dead trees, downed trees. Dying wood, all the dying wood, gnarled from living, now providing food for the Pileate and Downy Woodpeckers. A man can recharge, feel his youth surrounding him here. The birds and the ducks and the geese sing happy. Your worries seem less. Look at the eagle soaring."

I smiled, seeing Mr. Drazkowski emerge, and I remembered the quiet he carried. "Nice seeing you," I said

He smiled and nodded. "This refuge is eternal, like Heaven on earth. Out here and in the cabin was where I felt best. Mom and family made me whole. One with nature as should be."

I looked at him hearing the rippling sound of the Poplar leaves. Science Girl asked, "You see that hummingbird with the red neck and black head?

I told her no, and she started talking about their migration across the Gulf of Mexico to get to their winter home. 500 miles in one day, non-stop. Those little birds, I thought.

She said, "Let's get back to walking."

I heard Mr. Drazkowski whisper to take care of her. "She changed your living."

##

Blue Dream, Blue Dream. I was out walking the streets of Seattle. It was a nice day, the air felt fresh. Science Girl and I were vacationing in Seattle, and she told me she needed a break shortly after arriving. Told me to take a hike, find some dead people, and she would meet me at Shamble's Bar.

I didn't argue as I always like going for a walk. It helps me settle down, and I like nosing around. I thought when I saw this business called Heart to Heart, that I might find something for Science Girl. She has got some mystical leanings to her being and that Heart to Heart might have some books or something about an alternate world. I got talking to the counter girl. Name of Sara.

She said the Blue Dream can change a person's thinking. "Take the anxiety right out of you," she said. Anxiety, stress gone.

I got myself just a small stash when Sara said some folks start seeing things in a different light.

"Sure," I said, "We'll give it a try." I headed outside looking for the vibe. I started walking. I could feel the stash working, hearing the sounds of cousins and uncles talking. Dead grandparents and those who walked the trail long before I was born. I headed down the alley by the fruit market where folks who think differently are known to hang.

I had a good hour before meeting Science Girl so I decided

to sit on the stoop of the old brick building which might have been a bar or a restaurant in its long life. An apartment upstairs and a little step so I could sit and sample the Blue Dream.

I started hearing the wind and the old brick alley talking. That wind whispered, the leaves rustled as they flapped back and around. I felt the rush that a city brings as the energy of its people work through me.

"Hey, Hanson," I heard coming from a few stoops down.

I picked myself up, walking slowly.

She was wearing a polka dotted dress. Big White Polka Dots on a navy-blue dress coming down to near her ankles. Her face was all wrinkled and skin hung down low past her jaw line.

I asked her, real quiet, "How are you?"

I saw her long fingers that seemed to be near a foot long and nails that were sharp. I figured she must have been about 6 foot 4 and she wore old schoolmarm shoes.

"My name is Hannah." She had these pencil thin boobies reaching her waist. She looked at me and said, "I gave life to nine boys and three girls. The last boy didn't want to let go. Sucked me dry."

She said she was on the welcoming committee for those who walk the alleys of Seattle. She said it's nice to finally meet the man who sees and talks with the dead. "You'll find the finest people in Seattle, and they aren't all white and straight. Seattle has got heart," she said. "Remember us," she said, "as you make Seattle one of your homes away from home."

Gone she was and I decided I best get a move on walking the Blue Dream.

Madison, Wisconsin wakes my thinking. We stay at a Motel called the Ruby Marie. Just a street crossing to the lake where Otis Redding and his band called the Bar-Kats took their last breath as their plane crashed in the lake called Monona. Twenty-six Nobel Prize winners have roots on the campus and even Dick Cheney once walked its grounds..

It's easy to get lost in Madison. The roads don't run straight in this city built next to a lake. Bikers and walkers in every direction. I like getting lost, losing direction, but Madison is a short drive from Winona and Science Girl had said I needed to get out of town. The dead ones were starting to show up in her daily dealings. Sometimes we go North and I can breathe in the northern woods, but a city is a whole different beast.

We had been at the Athletic Club, listening to The Bus Boys and talking to Polish friends who'd I never met when she told me we were headed out of town. Time to see Hamilton, she said.

Hamilton is a story of an orphaned West Indies immigrant who rose to power during the revolution. He helped write the Federalist papers and designed our financial system as Secretary of the Treasury under George Washington. He died of a gun shot wound inflicted by the standing Vice President of the United States, Aaron Burr.

It was a marvelous play, a musical. I never thought this townie would like musicals but I keep learning. We walked back to the Motel. It was just a mile or so from the Overture Center. A beautiful night with a nice breeze coming from the lake. The Ruby Marie has an adjoining bar called the Up North Tavern. Just an elevator ride up to our room. Live music and this night they had bluegrass playing, something put together by a guy named Majestic. My townie heart was alive.

I was pretty much drunk, stoned, and happy as I stepped outside to get some fresh air after a set. I sat down on the stoop facing the Madison Oil and Gas Company. It wasn't long before some old guy looking mostly like hell on earth sat down with me, telling me the Ruby Marie had fallen into disrepair in the 70's and 80's. It had turned into a men's shelter. A place for the out of luck to lay their heads.

"If you listen to the woodwork, Hanson, you'll hear the sounds of life shattering. Many of us drank too much and our relations with women left something to be desired. This place was filled with guys barely alive. An eyesore in the neighborhood. Drunks, prostitutes, and fights. I lived through those times. In 1992 a guy by the name of Robert Worm started renovating the block building by building. You can feel it, Hanson, it was here that I spent my dying days."

I looked at him, seeing how time changes in all of its majesty. I thought back to old history teachers who piqued my interest in history and thought how much history is so much more than memorizing dates. I heard the band starting up inside and thought what a great country we live in. Peace.

Friends

I was staring at the large Fastenal building that now occupied the land where Charlie's Bar once stood. Stony Bridges was dead, and I was retracing some of the steps and alleys Stony and I used to walk. Stony was a few years older than me, but we knew each other from early on. We became closer in Charlie's Bar sipping Jack Daniels and Canadian Whiskey. We both heard the voices and folks like us don't often find kin.

We'd party all night and sleep in. Get up and get wasted again. Some of my learning, good and bad, has happened on those late drinking sprees. We'd find our stools and Dee would serve us a drink. Sometimes we didn't leave those stools except to go to the bathroom or have a smoke outside until the lights got turned down and the juke box shut off.

We would just head down the dimly lit street stopping on the stoop of Reinarts Glass Studio where we would light up whatever Stony Bridges was selling. It was 1978. The cop shop was close, but we'd discovered that in all their comings and goings they didn't pay any attention to what was nearly right in front of them.

"This is Zombie Wombie, Hanson. Over in the Coulees they

say in quiet tones that it's like talking to God himself. Those Hippies say a real peacefulness will settle you when you smoke this weed. No, no, this stuff relaxes your mind I tell you. You'll be wanting to do good things for people. Makes you feel good, like God has found its way into your being."

I looked at Stony Bridge. His beard was all matted and his hair was going every which way. It looked like a bird could make a nest in that mass of hair he carried on his face. His eyes were lit up like a 4th of July sky. I smiled and thought about 1978 and how much growing up I'd had yet to do.

Stony knew all the judges and cops and probation officers. He wasn't much good at mischief. He never got away with anything. Always caught and sent somewhere to get straightened out.

Seems his problem was he told everybody that he was going to steal something before he did it. His friends would try and stop him, but Stony he was a hardheaded man who refused to change. Change ran against his grain, his myth of being a man. Stony was set in his ways early.

Now Stony was never quiet about nothing. Walking, talking, eating, and burping. "Real men," he said, "don't change their thinking like the blowing wind."

"Stony, you ain't never had a straight thought in your head, and I've known you since I started kindergarten," I told him.

"My Daddy was a Marine," he said and he stuck out his chest and then dropped his shoulders. "Serious Marine. See a hill, climb it, plant a flag, never waver. Bullets can't stop a Marine."

The Zombie Wombie was filling my bones, and I didn't want to do much talking about guns and killing people. I was never a military man. Order has never been part of my thinking.

"Old Marines never stop the fight at the dying," he said. "No sir, we'll haunt the men who threw us in harm's way and nothing, nothing ever stopped a Marine. Not even death itself." Then he took a deep breath and mumbled something about a conscience. "I started hearing the voices soon as I got done with high school. It came on out of the blue, fast. Jumpy and fearful. Something wrong inside.

"I got accepted and then rejected by the Marines. Something about not being able to take orders and confusion. They didn't even think they could fix me, straighten me out. I had a panic to my being. I had signed up at 16 like my father before. Zombie Wombie, this weed settles the demons inside my thinking."

I told him that those demons were kind enough that they'd told me, "Guns and you don't match. You got a short attention span. You see and hear things most don't. Guns are a responsibility."

I just shook my head and let Stony carry on. "I got sent to Camp Pendleton nearly right after high school," he said. "Got sent back home within a month. A military reject at a time when the military was low on morale and esteem and numbers. I guess they got around to looking at my rap sheet and listened to my thinking. Demoralizing to get booted out of the Marines. I was ashamed, Hanson. Home was not home, as family looked, shook their heads and stared at me. Little cousins who once looked up to me had started sneering. I could hear the whispers coming out the woodwork.

"Ain't nothing wrong with him. He is just a coward, fearful, weak in his thinking. I let Dad down. I stopped going home."

I took another hit and felt the peace start settling in my thinking. Stony was talking about letting go of the pain attached to his own living. I nodded and said, "Some folks just ain't wired to be a Marine. Let's go have another. Takes a special brand of thinking to be in that branch."

I stood up and he followed. Darby had one waiting for us, and we allowed our thoughts to settle before opening our mouths.

We sat mostly quiet trying to slow our thinking. New surroundings send a mind spinning. The voices running through our heads were going every which way. I was worried about the smell a good weed can carry. The Zombie Wombie, didn't carry the smell some good pot does.

Some California geneticist must have figured a way to remove the smell trying to keep one step ahead of the good men wearing blue. I looked at Stony and he shook his head. His eyes were glassy and somewhere other than Charlie's D and D bar.

I remembered that old stink weed that sometimes made its way through town. That stuff was bad enough to have the neighbors call Dickey's Pest Control. Dead animal not to be found. That was nerve racking trying to get high and staying one step in front of the law. Had to get far away out in the woods, just to open your thinking. That stuff just lingered.

This old guy was staring at me from down at the end of the bar. He had a smoke hanging from his lips and he looked plain ornery. Looked like he was aiming for a fight and us Zombie Wombie boys weren't coherent enough to provide any resistance.

I nodded at him and motioned for Darby to buy him a beer as I asked him, "What was wrong in your world today?"

He stared at me over the top of his smoke and took a long drag. He blew out a billowing puff of smoke and said, "I don't like you pot smokers. Destroying the very fabric of this town, this country. You wonder why this country has gone down the tubes I'm staring at it. I should wring your necks."

I smiled. He was obviously itching for a fight and so if I was going to get my head beat in, I was doing it on my own terms. Stony had started giggling.

"It started in Nam, when you whiny kids started protesting. You're yellow is what you are," the old guy said.

I was surprised Stony didn't go flying over the bar attempting to kill the crusty old bastard right then and there. Nobody called Stony Bridges, yellow. Old Stone, had heart and though he wasn't able to serve he was all in when it came to fighting. Stony to my way of thinking was a casualty of war. His heart bled the colors, and he was all about America. That Zombie Wombie, might have saved both men's lives. Without it Stony would have killed him, no doubt about it. Then he'd be slowly dying in some prison.

I was getting ready to reply how it takes courage to stand up to the powers that be, but then he would've probably asked me outside and beat the living tar out of me. Like fists were the answer. I wondered what kind of demons this man had in him, when I heard Stony whisper that he had a Dark Columbian sitting just inside his beard.

Better than listening to some guy who had a bad day, a bad week, a bad life. That sure sounded like a better proposition than getting beat up, and so I nodded to Darby and said later.

We hadn't got to Reinart's stoop when Stony started yelling. "He is lucky I'd had some of this Zombie Wombie or he'd have been dead," he screamed. "Siebert, that cop, he'd be slapping the cuffs on me, and Judge Sawyer would be saying I'm headed to Stillwater. Who was that guy, Hanson?"

"An old townie, not happy with his living. Lashing out at whatever seems close. He's blind, Stony, trapped by all the hate running through him. A little weed would do him some good. Maybe we should bring some brownies the next time we go. A peace offering. Change his entire insides as he sees the ugliness of his being."

He pulled the joint out of his beard, pencil thin. He said, "This weed sometimes brings out the bugs."

"The bugs?"

"I've seen some folks take midnight swims trying to rid their skin of the bugs crawling on them. Some folks start itching hard enough to draw blood."

"So why would I smoke it Stony? It does what?"

"When it settles it's a glorious light high. 1% get the itches. I've found it worth it, but I can't decide for you."

He lit up the joint and hadn't started itching and being a firm believer that a man shouldn't drink or get high alone I allowed the Columbian to enter my being. I could feel my skin drying, my pores closing. My scalp started turning itchy, and I started frantically scratching my scalp.

"Breathe," Stony told me. "Deep breaths. Look, up at the magnificent sky hanging over Winona."

I felt the peace settle me in a way I'd found over the years to be the sign of fine, fine living. Quiet, comfortable and warm.

"We live in a remarkable place, Hanson. River, bluffs, songbirds singing, though the nighthawks have disappeared from our town. No place quite sounds like Winona in the stillness of night. All the energy bounding back and forth between the bluffs and the river providing white noise, allowing us to find quiet in the littlest of things.

"I'd a killed him, Hanson, without the Zombie. Damn soldiers, disease. My military experience gnaws at me. Gets in my bones, doesn't leave me. Sometimes you just snap, lose it, the stress comes bubbling up through you. Start yelling, screaming at imaginary things."

"Look at the stars. Millions of light years away. Why they might already be dead and we wouldn't know it. Funny, how light moves," I said.

Stony, he started laughing and telling me about the first time he got high at Stoner's Circle. All the boys were there.

I took another hit, stared at the sky, gave my thanks I wasn't carrying the baggage the dude in the bar was carrying inside his thinking and let the evening come over me.

##

Far too many of us think we know it all. Fact is, we are all a bit ignorant about some things. That's okay, you wouldn't want me handling a gun or driving a semi-truck or fixing anything mechanical. I don't do carpentry or plumbing or most anything very well that requires a different kind of thinking. Some of us just think differently and our blind spots are in different ways.

We like to think that the other guy doesn't think right. In our early years we hung with people who had a relaxed way about them. They were our friends and when I think back to high school and look around the cafeteria, I see nothing but people caught up in their own worlds, sharing ideas about their life and where the social gathering was on Friday night.

There are people who think discipline is the answer to our problems. Work harder, make more money, go to church, raise the flag are some of the things we do. Those folks who walk that talk still got problems and sometimes I think they spend too much time imposing their beliefs upon others.

I hear my friend Frankie say organized religion is the root of evil and that before there was religion there was a spirit, an energy. He keeps telling me to look at the stars. He says early man has been staring at that moon forever knowing there was something magical about the nature of it all. Even before written words, there was a spirit and he didn't see church or the Bible as a way to attain that spirit. Frank is dead, but I still hear his words and when I see his children and grandchildren, Frank is carrying on.

Myself, I don't go to church more than a couple times a year.

I find it noisy and the quiet time my body and mind needs doesn't get satisfied sitting in a church pew with fifty other equally distracted people. I find my needs met in the quiet sanctuary of the woods or even in an empty church on a winter afternoon. God have mercy some say, but the God I hear is just happy I found a way to enjoy the wonderful beauty in the center of us all.

We have become more superficial through the years. We have gotten away from the real meaning of man, thinking it is all about thy self. In the old days thyself took second in the eyes of most and the person who placed the importance of others in front of them was most respected.

As Christmas approaches, I think about the people who have left my life. I feel them, smell them and even sometimes hear them. My Grandpa has been dead for 50 years, but I felt something as I drove by the Minnieska Church last month.

I felt a calling to see the world through his eyes. I visited the pews and confessional booth and I stepped where he stepped so many years ago on his wedding day. I saw that river as I looked out the front doors from where he stood facing the pews as a married man. I saw old cousins wanting to get the party started and I saw happiness on most everyone's face. I saw my Grandma in her youth and heard the voices of 100 years of praying.

I was stoned beyond being able to carry on a conversation. I had come stumbling out of the Club Bar, needing fresh air and rest for my dancing legs. I could hear Geno the Wino as the door opened and closed.

Petey Hawaiian slipped me a joint. "Jamaican," he said.

I nodded saying, "For tomorrow's walk, I'm tired tonight. I don't feel like talking, socializing, nothing. Just want to put my head on a pillow."

It was 1979 and my world was upside down. I had to get out and away. The narrative going on inside my thinking was driving me.

I headed out for a walk that next morning and before I knew it, I was out by the old Deer Park. It was a beautiful fall day, and I was out sorting through my problems. Jamaican fueled my walking.

I passed the campground and noticed an old fellow tossing in a line out by the spillway. I put on my townie face and sauntered down to the riverbank to see what was biting.

Turns out he was a right nice fellow. Jerry was his name, and this was his first summer of fishing without his wife Helen. She'd passed during the winter.

"It was the hardest thing, not having a wake. I ain't got many years left and most of our friends are in the same boat. We all want to say goodbye before we go. The pandemic has been hard on us old folks.

"Used to be, We'd go visit Arkansas every winter. Fished every day. It's how we unwound. We'd talk about the kids, life, politics. I don't think you ever stop worrying about kids.

"It was cheap eating after all. I've had a piece of fish every day for the past 40 years, and I'm talking real fish not that fast food breaded fish. Helen had a garden, and we grew our own vegetables.

"I didn't plant a garden this spring. That was Helen's space. I was never much interested in weeding. Bad knees you know. She had one of the Mary statues in the back corner of the garden. Never one much for church. I'd find all the spirit I could ever ask for along this river."

"Fish don't seem to be biting," I said.

"Oh, I suppose if I had some bait on my hook the fish would be biting. Doesn't matter, but today, I'm searching for Helen. Fishing brought us together."

##

"I was back in the times of my beginning. My Mama must have been carrying me in her womb when Patsy Cline was number one on the radio. The is Stoner Thompson reporting the morning after from the old Kewpee Cafe.

"Me and Sal went to opening night of Always Patsy Cline at Winona's Great Shakespeare Festival. It was marvelous from start to finish. We took my mom and her two sisters. Patsy was the singer in the times of their life.

"Now they drove themselves and parking during the summer is easy on campus unlike the rest of town. Right on Belleview Street between Main and Huff. Walk a block or so and you are right in the center of campus. You don't even have to walk steps to gain entry to the DuFresne Center though most of us call it Vivian's place. That's nothing against President DuFresne and I might have met him once but Vivian Fusillo is one of a kind.

"Me and Sal took the long way to the play-concert, hotwiring that VW van that sits in Elmer's car lot up Fountain City way for our ride and did what children of the 60's and seventies used to do before a concert. Mom and her two sisters wanted nothing to do with my driving and certainly didn't have no interest in hot wiring that van. I told them their brother was probably going to catch a ride with us. He caught the Patsy bug early being the sisters were forever calling the radio station getting that disc jockey Melvin to play Patsy Cline.

"Sure, as shooting the minute, I set foot on campus I started hearing dead people talk. Larry Gorrell, retired now, told me he was all hot and bothered. All his bodily parts were feeling love for not only Patsy, played by Brittany Poira but Louise played by Tara Flanagan. Louise and Patsy make me feel like a man he said. I thanked my lucky stars. Living next to Larry was a trip.

"That's when Sal tapped me on the shoulder saying, 'Can't you stay in this world? At least wait till the singing, play-acting starts. It's like going alone sometimes. You're off in that delusional world of yours, talking to dead folks, and I'm all alone.' Thru the years I've learned to listen to Sal being time shows she's mostly right. Much easier when I don't get let my ego clutter my thinking.

"This is all brought to you by the fine sponsors of the Shakespeare Festival. I need a smoke break so kick back and enjoy. From 1957 here's Walking after Midnight."

##

You should have seen all the dead folk. Smiling and carrying on. They thought it was pretty cool how the class of 76 had a reunion every year. 46 years now. Old friends gathering.

Frank chimed in, "It's not so bad over here. Miss my friends. Life goes on. I'll be here when you get here."

The old guy next to him said, "I walk thru this bar every day. Not that any of you living folk can see. Go to mass, stop for a beer. Down there in the big church that used to be a little church. You're the first living person I've come across who can see the dead. Except for my Uncle Richard. He'd hang one on sometimes and claimed he saw God himself. Claimed a bright white light that blinded him. And then there was little Dickie. He smoked some of that Marijuana and acid in the 1960's and his thinking was never quite right after that. He saw a lot of things."

"How old are you?" I asked.

"Well I was born in 1803 and died in 1895. I never expected life to keep on living once that pine box closed. Church every day kept me going. Lived with my daughter and her husband Frank Stolpa. Trouble just seemed to find us. My name is John Remus."

I took a look around the happy bar. Nobody else was talking to Frank and if you knew Frank that was not common when living. Peri Burcalow said hi as she walked by saying she had story for me. LuLu, the bartender asked what we were drinking. I ordered two Patrons for Frank and myself. Ordered Remus some of that Pine Creek shine. Peri said she was off the sauce and all the other things that followed her when living.

LuLu said to John, "The only reason you went to church daily is you had the fear of hell running through you. You and your offspring were regular features in the Winona Republican Herald."

"Now you listen here Miss LuLu. Me and my kin didn't handle freedom well. We made choices, mostly bad ones but you take a look around Winona today. All these big companies owned and run by the Polish. We are part of this town and its history. Our misdoings helped form the character of the Polish immigrants, yesterday and today. We were still good people.

"Those journalists never much got past Franklin Avenue much less Old Stone road. How objective could they be when the only time they saw us was in the courts? They lift their noses while sitting in the comfort of a plush office. The east end was a world apart from the west end folk. Our actions tarnished many a good Polish family and at the core of being Polish is a goodness. This bar is full; ain't you got work to do?"

Frank and Peri started laughing and as I looked around the bar I started seeing old classmates who I hadn't seen in a good long while. I could feel myself breathing as the class that graduated on the 200th birthday of our country raised our glasses to lives lived. We walked out back, hearing happy voices at the Brickyard.

Illnesses Abound

My stomach just hasn't been feeling right. It matched my head, nose and chest. It was a bad year for the early fall cold.

I always try treating my colds with foods, figuring if I can adjust my insides, I'll get to feeling better. Usually, I'll do the hot peppers, or a good dose of wasabi and the cold will let go. It'll open up my eyes and nasal passages, get my eyes a watering, and my stomach starts turning in a different way. Old reliable took me to the bathroom but couldn't beat the virus running its course.

I don't think the dead folk much like being around somebody sick. They didn't show up in my thinking or my vision the whole times I was under the weather. Now I know they were still around because I could hear them carrying on beyond the seeing. Us not so quite right folks hear things most don't, but the voices I heard weren't quite clear.

That was when Drs. Barth and Perella came a calling. In a town where Pizza is king, these boys have been doing it for fifty years, long before the corporate boys showed up in this town along the Mississippi. You don't stay in the restaurant business for fifty years unless you got a good tasting product.

I eat Rocco's and Sammy's not as often as I used to, but if one of their pies don't make you smile, satisfy your cravings, or fix what ails you, then you best head to the hospital as there is something seriously wrong with you. The growth in the area just above my waist is the price I pay for satisfying my cravings and taste buds.

It didn't take too long before I could feel myself waking. I had myself a sausage, mushroom, extra cheese from Sammy's, and by the next morning I was taking an early morning walk hearing the pleasant sounds of birds chirping and seeing the trees wearing their best fall wardrobe. I could feel that virus just flying away as a good pizza worked its magic

"It's good you are back, Hanson." An old teacher said as I walked past. "Us dead folks were worried we had not a soul to talk with. It's the quiet, the quiet, on the other side of living that makes time what it is."

I turned and saw the wrinkly face of Miss Kathryn Dunlay. She had a full head of white hair and she dressed in the finest clothes with a strand of pearls bought at Morgan's. It was on the block called the Morgan Block long ago.

"I walked these streets every day to work," she said. "Fall is my favorite time. I can feel myself breathing, thinking, feeling. I taught at Phelps on the Winona State campus you know."

I nodded, remembering full well when I was a young lad and had her as a teacher. She helped me read, taught me to read between the lines. Her life was spent teaching and a good teacher makes all the difference. For that I am grateful.

She lived in the tan house on the corner of Sixth and Broadway. It was the home of bank president Mr. Risling and then Mr. Mahl, also a Bank President. Miss Dunlay inherited the house from the Mahl family. She tells me that house had life to its being. Mr. Mahl loved the piano, and she would play it every night before Mr. Mahl closed his eyes.

"He was no ordinary banker," she said.

We kept walking, caught up in the memories of yesterday. "Not so much traffic then," she said. "I lived for nearly a hundred years dying in 1999. I would have liked to live in three centuries, but I was late to the prior one and not long enough to the next one."

We started getting close to the campus. I told her my cold was telling me to sit for a spell, so I sat on that bench near the old library across from the Miller Brothers engineering building. She carried on, climbing the big steps to Phelps.

I sat a bit and heard the yipping of the Pomeranians barking outside the house where the Miller building now stands. A house full of life occupied by Carol, Rodney and Russell along with a few other Hoesley's that I never met.

I glanced at the superbly landscaped grounds, took a deep breath, and felt good about being alive. That's when I heard, "Hanson. My name is Henry Hull."

I smiled, knowing Professor Hull knew most everything and was entertaining to boot. Life is good, and I started listening.

##

I made it to the benches facing Phelps Grade School on the Winona State Campus. I was looking at the beautiful old building and remembered classmates, teachers and friends. Though the sounds of kids have left the playground, I still get a jolt when I think back when.

We saw Protesters and Picasso as we grew up in the space surrounded by a college. Here, surrounded by old friends the myth of America was planted in my thinking. A fine grade school it was.

We got taught the Patriotic songs early on by a music teacher named Carlis Anderson. Now I wasn't much of one for music, suffering from a mostly tin ear, but the songs all stirred my patriotic soul whether we sang This Land is your Land, The National Anthem, or America the Beautiful. We started each day with the pledge.

The nice thing about the educating we got is we got to learn about the people who wrote the songs that stir us yet today. Learning went a bit deeper at the Phelps Laboratory School. Katharine Bates, who wrote America the Beautiful, composed her song while riding a train through the Western States. Purple Mountain Majesties is like a picture. It was in the days before cars and taking the train was the least stressful way of seeing the country. Might still be, though I like the backroads.

Woody Guthrie rode the rails as a hobo and bum during the time of our great depression when hunger tore the American soul. Woody had way of seeing that appealed to many a folk. An attachment to their way of life and *This Land is your Land* still ripples through me.

Francis Scott Keyes wrote the Star Spangled Banner about a battered, beaten up, tattered, ripped old flag still standing at Ft. McHenry. He was on board a truce ship. He had no interest in fighting. That beaten up old flag spoke of an American way.

People protested the song and the militarism of killing and racism back then. Some folks said it was too hard to sing and that the later verses became not about the glorious flag but Keyes and his upper crust believing. America at its very core is about protest. Just who we are.

The song was written during the administration of James Madison who witnessed the burning of the President's house, the Treasury, and the Capital from across the Potomac. In fact, Keyes himself believed diplomacy could have avoided the War of 1812. History is not just a shiny flag and a fancy car, though they have written their share of history in their graying days as time slips from their grasp.

I'll never forget my first and only encounter with Henry Hull. He was a history professor from Winona State and came over to teach us for an hour or so about Minnesota History and in this case, milling. He knew everything about milling from the mechanics of grinding to the transferring of energy from the water to the grindstone. He told us of the Porter Mill and its burning down and of Rothwell and Garvin who started up the Bay State as memories of the Shangri La Motel and the CJ Maybury designed Methodist Church fires still danced in our young heads. I never saw an hour pass so fast as Henry Hull raced across the chalkboard, chalk flying and dust trailing his very footsteps. We used to go for walks around campus. Those old houses smelled of history and money as we learned history on the very old sidewalks of Winona town. Life in a boom town, a lumber town, a train town, the early myths still beat in this Phelps boy soul.

Thank you, teachers, for showing me the story of a great, great town.

##

I've heard voices forever and feel fortunate I've lived in this river valley most of my 61 years. I rode my bike, walked, and later drove. I always felt rushed driving, or biking, and or even walking on Fifth and Sixth, so Seventh is what I took.

A life spent listening to the whispers of yesterday all along that street from this west end boy. The words from the shadows have been mostly comforting, but the honesty of the dead can be a bit terrifying as they question most everything. Every house in this town has stories and myths attached to its history, dark deeds, good deeds and all in between. And for those of us with the disease they all whisper.

Some days I go visit the nuns as they go about their day. They seem mostly happy, and I'm not certain that was always the case as they educated students who were sometimes sent from the mansions out East to tame the wild, restless spirit that had taken overtaken their daughters. Some good learning took place in those chambers of learning where history bounced in their words and off the walls.

They tell me their thinking has grown deeper as time changed light. I look at them and feel my inner Winona, wanting to know, to question another person and their way of thinking. I wonder about the light and how my perceptions about the other side of living seem deeper than what I once thought.

That's when I started coughing as the ugly traces of the 2020 flu sprouted out of me. Another day of that and I think I might have been dead. I'm done not getting a flu shot. I raised my finger to the ladies of the past, my dry cough getting in the way of my talking as I pointed my index fingers to the heavens, saying I'd be back, my energy is low.

I heard the low dark rumbles of the Mansion, now a park where the Bishop, and all his merry men played their game and knew I needed to get stronger.

##

I had quarantined myself up. Not seeing anyone or doing anything except for walking in the woods, buying some eating supplies, and making sure Mom was still eating.

It was late afternoon when I decided to pour myself an absinthe. I got the hot water and the sugar cube all set up and began wondering where I was soon headed. The voices started talking. It wasn't in-your-face talking but the subtle whispers of those beyond the seeing.

I heard old priests saying God was angry and mad, while other priests whispered the devil was asserting his way, filling us with delusions every step we took. They claimed the whole world has fallen to the Devil seed, and I heard the words of Father Dan Dernek saying the house of God, his mansion, is the river and its bottoms and its changing story and landscape.

"Do you see how ill prepared you are?" the wise men scream. "How can you think that guns will keep you safe or that sending money to TV preachers who live in castles and dance with snakes promising you, that only their way can get you to the promised land. Trapped in your narrative, leaving you blind to fight the demons all around us." Their voices sank into whispers.

I took another sip of the absinthe. Tried collecting my thoughts as the world spun around. A thousand voices rolling out from nowhere all rattling inside my head as I assessed myself in the light of a casket closing. Time it keeps ticking and waits for no one.

The absinthe, I thought as the grey-haired squirrel started telling me that young squirrels have gone soft, eating the scraps of man like the city squirrels do.

"I never much cared for the eating habits of men," the sassy squirrel said.

I stared.

"So eating, what they don't eat I find repulsive. Us old squirrels worked for our food and hid nuts for later. I hear from some of my cousins who live in the woods that the trees aren't looking too well as man keeps invading their homeland. We understand your need for food, and we'll pay the ultimate price if things get bad, but nobody knows how to cook squirrel like your grandma did. No sir, no sir, a lost art. Cook us well, cook us well.

I looked at the absinthe thinking maybe I'd drunk enough, and at least for today put the absinthe down.

##

Hope everyone is safe. I have a son living in NY and a daughter in Seattle. We used to joke they got as far away from the old man as they could. I wish they were closer.

It was a sad day for many of us. Long time, friend and Winona Legend Stoner Thompson had passed on. I was sitting in the No Name Bar passing time.

I grew up with Stoner, fishing and playing ball. We baked brownies in Ma Arndt's Home Economics class, and everybody seemed happy, carefree in the times of innocence.

We would go out driving, cruising to pass time. Gas was 19 cents a gallon and my Volkswagen Bug made for some nice road trips. We'd drive past Stone Circle and Woodlawn Cemetery, turning down Huff and we would stop into Papa John's for a sausage, mushroom, extra cheese pizza. Old man Rickoff made a nice pie that satisfied our munchies, and back then calories just seemed to disappear.

Hard to believe he is gone, I thought as I downed the Corn Whiskey. After high school we had gone our separate ways. Stoner served his country joining the Army like his father before, and I took the bumpy path of college. Different roads to manhood.

I looked around the Sportsmen Tap as it used to be called. The walls were full of local art and the live music played in the bar had made it a must stop for musicians looking to make a living doing what they loved. Back in our innocent years, Stoner would get to talking about living after dying, and I half expected him to come rolling out of the woodwork.

I saw no Stoner today, but I could feel the memories of what we had rumbling through me. The time we had together was a big part of who I became. I always thought Stoner would grow old and die like people used to, never thinking a bug from a faraway place would do the deed.

Life doesn't turn out like we planned in the days of innocence. No life is full of turns and twists that don't always work. I settled my tab, stepped outside looking for a bench to sit on. I thought about Stoner as I let go and wondered if he found living after dying. Peace Brother.

##

I was walking in the cemetery. St. Mary's. Visiting my Dad. It was the birthday of my youngest son who lives in Brooklyn.

He moved out to New York shortly after graduating. About ten years. All holed up in a new, clean condominium with his beautiful, lovely wife. They got their computers, their music, their work. And the restaurants, any food you want. Subways only get you so close, so you walk.

"Not easy being the youngest," Dad said. "Brothers and sisters telling you what to do. They all usually love you but finding your own voice ain't easy. Some never leave home."

I looked at him when he said, "You have to live. See what's different. When you finally get here the light bulb will come on. No hurry but stay one step ahead of that bug. It seems to like older folks. An appetite that doesn't seem to get satisfied."

"Hey, I think you would be proud of your grandson, Dad. You know he has vacationed in Iceland and spent two weeks in Japan bumming, hiking around the country. On vacation! He makes me proud. You suppose it's changed since you were there?"

He lit right up with that beaming, goofy Hanson smile saying, "Japan," as he shook his head back and forth. "I was bored out of my senses watching the thirty ninth parallel. That weekend pass was freedom. That's where I got my tattoo, pointing to the snarling tiger on his forearm. I couldn't even tell you the city or town I was in. I was more than ready to leave the Marine Corps when my stint was done."

I looked out over the cemetery; the flag was gently blowing. People lined up to talk. Some I knew, some I'd heard of, and some were strangers to my seeing. Dad lit his pipe. I could see he had started drifting to another time. We nodded and I got up to leave.

He said, "Wish Jake a Happy Birthday. Tell him old gramps made out just fine."

##

Sad, sad times playing on that movie screen called TV. Cities burning, a generation getting wiped out by a bug we can't see and life seems mostly unhappy. I don't think I'll miss the hate when gone but then who knows what happens when this world ends.

I think I'll shut the TV off and go back to reading like my forefathers did. Don't need that nonsense the news has begun spewing. News isn't news anymore and Walter Cronkite is crying.

I wonder if the whole picture reveals itself on that other side. I'd been reading Thomas Merton, the pacifist priest that entered an abbey with a vow of silence during the chaos of his times. Merton reads deep and slow as every word has meaning. My last thoughts before sleeping.

The good, the bad and the ugly were leaving my body as a good night sleep recharges me. Thinking you know my rules it roared, and a loud laugh bellowed out of the rather large being. Not man, not women as that great spirit bellowed, "Preposterous."

I nodded and looked at the spirit. Is he male or female, animal or a beast? He looked different no matter how I looked, never the same twice.

"The face of all," the spirit said. "Not some grumpy old man who rules from on high. I am not angry at my creation. I gave you a brain to think. A mind to see. Nobody is the same. So how can you march to the same drummer, unless of course the devil planted the seeds of follow me, march in step, yes sir, no sir in your being."

The birds morning song woke me. I woke restless; my bones felt tense. This dream stuck. I don't usually remember dreams, but this one found its way to morning. They say dreams happen a couple times a night in everybody. The words of Merton triggered my dreams.

Science Girl and I had a talk last night about dying. I mean we are of the age where the bug starts seeing us as appealing. The poor girl carries some baggage in her thinking. I'm not the only one in this relationship with issues, but she says to me when it comes to dying, she might want to go out in a winter storm with me holding her hand and that how she wants to die is of her own choosing.

I nod my head thinking, whatever you want, I'll take your hand. Love, it sure rolls funny.

I got the pot a percolating, trying to sort through the thoughts of my standing when I noticed my Uncle Wayne had shown up in my living room. Dead folks have a way of stopping in. I poured him a cup and said let's step outside so Science Girl can finish her sleep.

The man had heart and I don't think it ever left him. No, even in death he has a way of handling himself. Deep down he is one of the finer men I've met. I was lucky to call him Uncle.

Decency was his middle name. Men like him don't make the front page of newspapers or TV news. Lots of things wrong in this world and integrity is in short supply. Integrity oozed out of Uncle Wayne Kramer and his every pore.

He was a working man, a truck driver, who drove tens of thousands upon thousands of miles hauling goods from coast to coast. Home was never far from the good-hearted man.

He and Lois worked together raising two fine children, Kurt and Karmen. Wayne, he was happy watching the grandkids play ball or heading across the river to watch the races around an old oval speedway. Family drove Wayne.

I asked him what life is like on the other side, and he had this funny way of laughing. His shoulders would kind of hunch, and he tucked his hands underneath his legs rocking back and forth. His laugh was contagious, and his blue eyes made everything better. "It's a surprise," he said, "like opening Christmas presents."

"My little brother is taking his last breaths. I didn't know it till I got here but it's a Kramer tradition to be there like my Pa was for me. I'll be waiting for Lois when her day comes.

"The family got together last week. I reached out, touched, and talked as we worked to clean up Darrel's yard of old cars and car parts, relics of yesterday. Most don't hear the sound of the dead, and my family is no exception, but it was nice to see them as one and I tried getting their attention.

"You can tell them, Hanson, that another life is just beyond the seeing and to live and love for as long as they breathe. Live life; dying can wait," he said as he left. "I'm going home."

##

I was going nuts. Four walls talking back to me every day. Pandemic. Nowhere to go. People walking around preparing for a funeral. Little bug we can't see. It doesn't seem in no hurry, plenty of food to gnaw on.

I needed to get away. Stare at something different, stop repeating the same lines. State Parks and camping grounds booked solid. Sanity starting to slip as the dead roared, demanding their story be written.

I felt my Daddy rising. I can't force stories to just pop out. I feel them in my bones, my knees, my head, my heart. Science Girl told me she found this nice little place right along the Mississippi. Brownsville, Mn.

I sat staring out at the river from the deck outside our room, I started feeling a relaxing coming. All the things I carry inside were letting go. A story, a story was coming, My body was releasing itself from the thoughts blocking my thinking.

There was an owl outside, hooting in the woods from right close. An awakening sound not heard often as I began drifting to a different place. Birds chirping, diving, swooning just outside my bedroom door and the mighty river kept rolling.

The dead folks seem happy here in Brownsville. I'm winding down my day having good thoughts. These are good people as laughter and serious talks echo in the pictures and shadows of lives well lived.

We had a fine, fine breakfast that next morning. Healthy muffins, some nuts, and orange juice. Felt alive, awake and alert. Thank you, Sharon, for sharing your home, your history, and the kindness that surrounds you.

Mourning

It's fall. A time for remembering. A time for cemeteries and old neighborhoods, old haunts.

The cold starts setting in and bones I've forgotten about start creaking, reminding me of yesterday when time seemed endless, and death was a far-away thing to my living. Time keeps ticking and that casket seems closer as the friends from my youth call it home and get to see the light in a different way.

I hear my grandparents in the falling leaves of the seasons changing. Fleeting memories of time long ago, moving slower, hearing the whispers in my walks as the old places crop up in my thinking. I search for old restaurants where my grandpa might have sat drinking coffee and having a smoke and realize far too many of the old places are now just yellowed archives.

My phone rang. It was Stoner. I sat down on the stoop of St. Stan's across the street from where old friend Riff once lived. Stoner said he had been out and about all summer. Talking and socializing with people all up and down the river.

"It's community," he said, "People searching for a place, putting aside their differences and gathering." He told me it's happening all over but he noticed it at the Polish Festival this year. "The Polish heart is back," he said.

"You mean like the Polka?" I asked.

He said, "No, no, their hearts are singing and happy, telling stories of their past and remembering the happy times when things, outside things, didn't stop the talking. A letting go is going on."

I asked how the battle was going, and he said the summer had been good. Nothing he couldn't handle. He and Cindy were doing fine, and he asked me if I wanted to get together for a beer down at the Athletic Club. I asked if that was a place where an Irishman might feel comfortable. He said he wasn't certain where a man came from had anything to do with it.

I got quiet remembering the demons running through me and how the dark clouds of my living made talk mostly impossible for periods in my life. When you got dead folks talking in both your ears, it makes talking to a living person difficult, a different reality than the one I was carrying between my ears.

I took a deep breath and told Stoner I'd meet up with him on Friday to see for myself if the East End was breathing. The phone clicked, I took a deep breath and felt the dead entering the church to hear the Gregorian chants that were taking place inside the Basilica called St. Stan's on a cold fall day.

##

"Hey, this is Stoner Thompson for the Ocooch Mountain Music Radio Show. The boys play all the best music down there on Third Street in Winona. All digital, clear as a whistle, no radio towers and the app is free.

"Now even though Hanson told of my dying a story or two back, you didn't think I'd leave my good friends just like that do you? Most of us have been through hell and high water to finally get to gray hair status and a person just doesn't walk, fly away from that. Grade school and high school chums stick through thick and thin, and death is no exception in the town I'm from.

"I've been out and about visiting you. With this coronavirus going around it's quite easy, and I find most of you sitting in front of the television set. I find it refreshing to see some of you have turned off the 24 hour "news" and found some good, decent things to watch. TV people and the news folk who feed us the garbage information are downright ugly.

"It gets lonely on this side of living and I've screamed, yelled, and danced in your living room old friends while you sit. Some good news is I ran into Slinky Sally. I hadn't seen Sally since the Allman Brothers played in the Minneapolis Armory back in the late 60's. The place was rocking, a wave of energy taking me away.

"That was the last we saw of each other. I went to serve my country in Nam shortly after and she started growing organic foods and living off the land out there in Wiscoy Valley. I thought of her often, but things kept getting in the way of me calling her. She passed a few years back and I didn't make her funeral.

"We started talking on this side, deciding to take a cruise. We hotwired the VW microbus out there at Winona Rentals and decided to go on a road trip. We headed up Stockton way and for the next few hours meandered the backroads, the small towns, valleys and ridges while listing to the songs that resembled the ones we drank, smoked and danced to back in the day."

##

It was a regular gathering of the Dead Professors Society, St. Mary's branch. It was normally a quiet affair where old men and women shared stories of old students and families.

Tonight as I walked into the Cardinal Club, the place was packed, and the voices were loud. What was usually just a muffin and coffee type of affair had turned into a boisterous gathering.

Brother Richard Gerlach was bartending. He had graduated from the school in its early days and had spent his life teaching at the high school level and then the University. He liked his hooch. I decided to sit at the bar.

"How's it going Brother Richard?" I asked.

"Damn world is falling apart. I saw the signs while still living. Falling apart." He poured himself a drink. Buffalo Trace Bourbon. He still moved awkwardly.

Not much different than when he was living so I asked him if he was still swimming on that other side. Brother Richard was a powerful swimmer.

"Dead folks don't swim. We float. It's a sad day, Hanson. The heart and soul of LaSallian studies cut. The sword of time turning everything into dollars and cents. Money, the devil's tool.

I asked him for a glass of Champagne, and he looked at me.

"Champagne on a such a sad day?" he asked.

"Trying to find the roots of our great school. St. John Baptiste De LaSalle and his mother's fortune had its roots in Champagne. Part of De LaSalle's identity."

He poured himself another. Man, he could drink.

"He saw the futility, the disconnect between the high-class French and us peasants who spoke the same language in an entirely different way. Education was given using the language of the elitists. Kids would come home to study and their parents knew nothing of the language and that way. The festering seeds of revolution. Cheers," I roared.

The Dead Professors Society stopped talking.

They were all staring. Fitz and Floody. Walt Ayotte and Father Fabian. Brother Finbar and Tom Etten. Father Taylor and Marietta Conroy. Brother Charles and a bunch of folks I'd never met.

Dead Professors whose life and teachings embodied St. Mary's enjoying coffee, drinks and finger food on a sad day. It was the Saturday after the school had announced it was cutting so many of the majors that helped form the St. Mary's identity.

Finally, Brother Frank Walsh squawked, "Didn't you get booted out of St. Mary's?"

I could feel all eyes turning towards me. I had Brother Frank for Political Science. It was ninety minutes of agony. He had a tone to his voice that would send this schizophrenic's mind into a different place. When he started talking, my mind went elsewhere.

Reminded me of being a kid and hearing the priest condemning us to hell. I'd felt comfort in staring out the stained-glass windows, thinking about anything other than the message coming from the pulpit.

I nodded. "Deservedly so Brother Frank. I didn't speak the

same language as you. I spoke schizophrenic and you spoke learned wisdom. I heard you though, Frank. The messages I heard coming out of all your and your colleague's mouths I still carry with me today. I'm 63 years old and none of you thought you would ever talk to a living person again, but your message resonates in my heart. Thank you."

"Were you seeing the dead when you were a student?" Dr. Johnson asked.

"Shadows," I said. "But I could feel you dead folk from a long way off. Getting to see beyond the seeing with any degree of clarity wasn't easy. Unnerving to be honest."

Brother Richard poured himself another bourbon, and I saw bottles of wine being opened at all the tables.

My body felt like moving. My body sits too long, and it becomes tight, uncomfortable. Lots of things wrong with my being other than my thinking.

I started looking at the walls looking for the pictures of yesterday. Noticed the cameras watching my movement. The security boys laughing at Hanson talking to air. Leave me alone I implored. Doing no harm.

I felt a nudge. One of the brothers wearing the full dress long black robe. And a baseball hat. SMC emblazoned on the cap wearing dorky black glasses.

"It was hard, Hanson. Reaching this other side and realizing there were dead people all around me that I didn't see when living. Missed opportunity. I could have done and learned much more. We never met. George Pahl. Brother George."

I nodded. Brother George had his picture on the walls of St. Mary's Hall. Brother George was before my time. One of those characters who still echoed on the grounds of St. Mary's long after his dying. He used to bring his glove to games played on Max Molock Field. He was also the school President and a Science Professor in his training.

"Is Max around?" I asked.

"He's out helping run the track meet. Max was good at all sports. He could have been a great hockey player you know. Just the way he was built. Baseball was his love. It was one of the things us brothers did was listen to baseball games on the radio. We loved baseball up on the hill and had radio antennas on Heffron and St. Mary's Halls. Max and baseball gave St. Mary's an identity.

"In the early days we were all about boys becoming men. We got a lot of students from Chicago early on. Many came from wealthy parents who thought education made for a better world. They thought getting a college degree was important in making the world a better place. Many were worried their children were spoiled by the money they had. Wanted us to make them men. Make them human. Make them compassionate. Grow them up. They don't listen to us."

St. Mary's was a Men's College until the seventies when that wall came tumbling down. Brother Charles would supposedly before teaching students biology and botany have them drop their drawers and show them how to wipe their butt. It was a different world yesterday when schools were more than memorization.

Brother George looked at me and asked, "How is it you are able to see us and talk with us?"

##

I was saying goodbye, letting go the grieving and trying to put words to my feelings.

Stoner was a good man, a good friend who came home. He came back from the war a different man than the one who enlisted.

I looked at a room full of men and women all carrying stories of their lives with Albert Thompson. The old boys of the VFW and Legion filled the seats of the funeral parlor. Old friends and faces I hadn't seen in years.

It's hard watching the demons come flying out of a man. Some say those voices weren't real. I saw my friend Stoner change before my eyes, taken by something I wasn't seeing nor hearing. Can't imagine hearing the whispers of dying, bullets flying, and the cries of life leaving. A lesser man would have died long ago.

We first bonded when we started riding our bikes to the lake and the river, searching for the big one that once got away. Catching Sunfish and having our moms fry them up. Fishing was everything till Nam for Stoner. He was a regular guy like us. We'd sneak out that 4th street door by the auditorium and start heading to the Hurry Back. Nobody cared. It was our time of care-free. A time where people left you alone. Everything wasn't an issue. Win some, lose some, go fishing.

I remember when he met Sally. I think it was the eighth grade. A whole new world opened up, for my friend. In his dying moments he told me Sal, that you were his greatest and only love. Thank you, Sal, for the light you were in Stoner's living.

About a month ago Stoner and I met at the Legion. We'd grown older. Our hair now white and our lives shaped by life and its rendering. As we sat trying to piece our lives together, Stoner looked at me and said Last Call.

Stoner and his honesty shone thru in the darkest of times. Just how he rolled. Made me a better man, so I asked him if he'd like to go fishing.

"Not in 40 years," He said, shaking his head. "The quiet, the peace, the gentle bob of a fishing boat gets me a thinking. Thinking about death, dying, and what might have been. Things I'm trying to forget," he said.

I took a deep breath trying to let the spirit of Stoner leave me. Thanks Stoner.

"This is Stoner Thompson reporting for the Ocooch Mountain Radio Show. It's been a crazy year even for a guy like me. I'm sitting here at the Kato Bar writing a commencement address for the class of 2021.

"Now I never in my wildest imagination did I think I might have to give a commencement speech. You see by all standards, I'm a failure. Broken down with no money. Near 65 and my body don't quite work like it used to. My mind is not only forgetful, but it has a hard time thinking in a normal direction. Now I could carry on and tell you I see dead folks and wake up at night with the sounds of war, smelling the Jungle and Napalm, but that's about me and this night is about you.

"You see the night of graduation is the last call, the last

roundup, for a group of people who have been together, sharing days of learning for the last twelve years. You've spent nearly as much time with your classmates as your parents. You share a town and memories and history, and in a fair world you should get a chance to walk across the stage like those before. It's a special night under the evening skies. Don't let anybody tell you it isn't a special night.

"Now it wasn't that long ago that I sat, like you're sitting listening to commencement addresses from my classmates. They used the right words with meaning and didn't seem very nerved up when they talked. Self-confident. Smart, gosh they were smart and one evening before the stars showed they spoke of aspiring to something better. Their message holds true yet today.

"Even though my world crumbled, fell apart on more than a few occasions, I tried every day to be a better human. Now I was never a great student. In Chemistry and Physics, subjects I didn't understand, I was poor. I couldn't see those things that were beyond my seeing. I even used to blame the teachers for my closed mind. How they worked, how they taught. I was fortunate to have had a science teacher who blew things up just to keep me awake.

"After graduating I went into the service like my uncles and fathers and grandfathers did before. They had come back normal from my seeing and military service is a respected choice in the Thompson clan.

"I came back a different man. The boy I was once had come back a broken man. One year in and I received a less than honorable discharge. My time in the army stuck to me like napalm on a burning body.

"I couldn't shake the war. A bundle of nerves and disconnected thoughts. I'd wake in the cold sweats, seeing the jungle, and smelling the fuel oil, burning napalm as if I were still there. No escaping that war. I'm guessing I'll be carrying it to the grave.

"Back in the days when Liz, Mike, Tim, and Sharon gave our high school commencement speech, I could not have foreseen how life was about to fall on my head. It does that sometimes.

"The point is when you leave tonight you will embark on a grand and glorious journey. You have a fresh start awaiting you to change this world, make it a better place, a more humane one.

We lost that in today's world. My generation stopped giving a damn somewhere along the way.

"You are now an adult in the eyes of most except for maybe your Mama who will forever see you as her baby. Step outside the lines and the local constables and judges will get to know you on a first name basis. There is nothing like a clanging jail door to bring you to your senses. Learning continues all through your life, and it seems as I sit here talking to you that those who keep learning, stay active and engaged do better in that game called life.

"Now and then I think about old teachers, most of them dead, and I realize how much they were part of my growing up. I thank them and honor them even though they didn't give me A's. That science teacher tried to explain to me how gases like hydrogen and oxygen bond, hold together, beyond my seeing to form water.

"Change the world, change the narrative. Be not afraid and when you get knocked down get back up. Follow your heart and travel, see other places, other people and be kind to your neighbors especially those who think different, act different. Make the world a better place. Never, ever stop fighting for human decency.

Welcome to adulthood class of 2021.

##

Me and my family have been fighting since the revolution and if I'd get around to searching, I'm guessing we were fighting in Europe before we came here. Poor folks fighting the king and his occupation.

I was doing my annual cemetery walk up next to the bluffs which the dead Catholics call home. It was fall, the skeeters had all died, and the sun was still hanging round till near 7. 'Bout near perfect weather.

The voices started up quietly. Joe's voice came in clear. "I served in WW1 and after I got done with my European tour I wanted nothing to do with war. I wanted to work, get married, raise a family and forget the three years of killing. It ain't easy forgetting, and forgiving ain't something I'm good at.

"It was a war of hates. Those folks had been at each other's throats long before we came into being. You could feel the hate in the air. I had friends who didn't return. I'd do about anything to have that smoke and a beer you are having."

I nodded my head, thinking sometimes a cold beer is good as it gets. I'd brought a lawn chair, hoping to listen to the sounds of yesterday. Joe started talking before I had hardly unfolded my chair.

He went on. "I never smoked before the Army. Never smoked in boot camp. But when I saw that first dead body up close, scattered remnants of bloody flesh strewn upon the ground I started smoking. Blood splattered all over. You smell death. You taste death and you feel death. Gets inside you. Death all around. You ever seen that, Hanson?"

I shook my head. Me and guns don't get along. Guns are a responsibility and with my attention span and forgetting problem I shouldn't have a gun. World is safer. No accidental killings or shootings. One less gun.

Joe sighed and kept talking. "I went to work. Had to work. You see it was my way of living with the war. Six days a week. Sixteen-hour days, more if I could get them. Put food on the table. Had five kids. I wasn't the best dad.

"They do that Hanson. The seeds of war, the devil's fruit bloom long after the guns stop. They drove me to work. I didn't want to hear those sounds and when I stopped moving, I heard the sounds of war like I was right there. I was a better grandpa.

"I should have talked, told more stories but when it came to the war, I couldn't put two and two together. I learned to trust my priest at St. Mary's where Roger Bacon Hall now stands. It was a quiet, reflective church, and I felt better after meeting my obligation. I wasn't much for that heaven and hell sermon.

"I'd seen hell as far as I was concerned but the priest would get a talking sometimes about soldiering. I had conditioned myself to block out the ways of war. War is so horrid that the men of war are driven by peace. I remember Father Sherman saying that the soldiers of war didn't want their sons to see war, to fight war. We fought to make the world a better place, Hanson, hoping this would be the last one."

I looked at Joe and slowly took a drag of my smoke. I could hear the sound of semis traveling down Highway 61 and thought how much quieter things used to be.

I'm not certain how Joe would handle today's world where the sounds and winds of war swirl no matter which way you turn. Could he find work to escape? Could he find space to forget? Could he find space to forgive? I felt the old ways of war dying each time a plane dropped a bomb with the push of a button and felt the sadness that a generation was growing up not understanding the grit and kindness of an old soldier.

Sitting in that cemetery, I started wondering what it's like being dead when Ed Pitowski started up talking. I had never met Ed, but that's the thing about dead folks; they enjoy company.

"Death didn't land hard as I thought it would," he said. "I heard the sermons you know. In one ear and out the other, but lingering thoughts of hell followed my entire living."

I smiled and thought of my own days sitting in the nice pews of the Catholic Church located in the west end of town, St. Mary's. It was kind and laid back and not quite like the strict learning of St. Stan's and St. Casmir's. Those Polish immigrants were serious people, especially about their churching. They tithed to build that church when a dollar was hard to come by. Serious people, who have been involved in the formation of many of Winona's largest companies.

Ed kept on talking. "You see I grew up down there by the Rudnik's and Riska's. Fairly close to the river and Gabrych Park. It was the other side of Mankato Avenue so there were nights when the air was tinged with the smells of the Swift meat packing plant located down there where Peerless Chain is now standing. It was the best playground in the world.

"I mean, I just didn't take to religion. Early on I found school wasn't at all for me either. I would get restless in tiny spaces, small rooms, felt like everything was closing in. I'd sleep outside in my tent during the summer, falling asleep to a campfire every night and in the winter, I'd crack the window open a good three inches. Neighbor kids said there was something wrong with me and we'd go duke it out under the big green stands of Gabrych Park.

"Ma and Pa knew early on I wasn't quite right, and I'd hear

them now and then wondering how best to raise me. They must have hoped that the Catholic educating would straighten me out, but no matter how hard Sister Polly pounded my knuckles and Father Beyewsezski roared about hell being the place for me, I never found learning in school. I dropped out in the ninth grade, never looking back.

"There were days when I'd walk in the front door of St. Stans school and right out the back. Head down to the foot of St Charles Street where the boathouses were. Tom Mikowskis gave me his keys to his boathouse, and he hung the boat keys on the wall. I was all of thirteen when I fell in love with the Mississippi river.

"Tom was a gentle man. He loved the river. He did most of his fishing in the evening. He once told me it stretched his days out and that the rolling current worked out the daily problems living brings about. Settled my mind," he said. "It didn't take me long to figure out that a day out on the river was better than swollen knuckles and math class. I regret few things, Hanson, in my long life, but I was serving my country in Korea when I got the news Tom died. I regret not paying my last respects."

I took a long sip of my beer realizing the tiny sacrifices taken by the men and women who serve our country. The Republican Herald used to list all the people serving and where they were at. People would write letters, heartfelt letters, to the boys serving. Lost America, I thought as that sun slowly set on another day.

##

"It was 1941. Thanksgiving Day. The thirties had been a rough decade. We grew watermelons and vegetables in that sandy soil and our land ran from the Mississippi River to Bolers Lake. Sold lots for home building. We worked our way through that dark decade. The Davis way," said Mrs. Davis.

"They were depressing times. Hungry kids and men wanting to work and no work to be found. We were about a year removed from Armistice day. Hundreds of duck hunters died out there on the river and the dust bowl was still on everyone's mind.

"War was the talk of the times from New York to Winona to California. Hitler had started his killing spree in Europe and Japan was just a few weeks away from hitting Pearl Harbor. The radio and the newspaper was, how we got our news. Gloom seemed to have filled the American spirit.

"Grandpa's seeing of course was mostly gone. He insisted on working until the last six months of his living. He'd get up in the morning, blind as a bat and start chopping wood. He liked getting his day started with physical activity. I prayed every time he lifted that ax handle that it wouldn't be the last. He died in 1946.

"I remember that holiday because Allen was coming home from his teaching position in Bertram, Minnesota. Roberta and Kenneth came back from Purdue University. Rebecca's William was getting to meet the family. Marion was already teaching down at Winona State and William, our son had gotten a leave from the Marine Corp. Our last Thanksgiving.

"The kids were all Grandpa and I talked about leading up to their arrival. They started showing up the night before and we had so much fun listening to them poke and jab each other. They were all up helping Thanksgiving morning. William said it felt good but strange being out of uniform. He had found his calling and that makes a parent proud. I noticed Allen was asking him lots of questions about being in the military. That night he told the whole family he was thinking about enlisting.

Soon after December 7, 1941 he joined the Army and spent his long military career studying weather and patterns. Allen was smart, and I wouldn't be surprised if he was part of the team trying to figure out the weather for the landing at Normandy. We didn't talk about war after 1944.

Son-in-law Kenneth was the smartest man I ever met. He couldn't tie his own shoes but he could play chess blindfolded and beat most everyone. He told me he once met Einstein in his latter days and worked at the Princeton Physics Laboratory much of his life. He was into harnessing the nuclear atom, and he would use big words sometimes I just didn't understand. Roberta kept him upright. Kenneth was a cryptographer based out of London during the war. He worked with Turing.

Marion brought life and energy to everything she did. It just ran through her and if one of the boys did something she was more than likely going to do something better. Bill he never made it home, dying in the South Pacific.

##

"It was shortly after that Thanksgiving. Marion had gotten some large maps of Europe and the far east from Winona State College. We hung the maps, on the walls of the dining room. Large, large maps so Pa could see how the war was going. He would mark the German movements with red pins, pushing the pin and whispering words that grandchildren can't use. The Japanese movement was marked by green pins. Grandpa was never much one for swearing but Hitler could get Francis Davis swearing with the best. He had skin fighting and dying in the South Pacific, fighting the devil who was messing with people and their freedoms.

"Grandpa Francis had that way of thinking. He had his issues like all men do but our marriage added meaning to my living. He never stopped thinking, never thought he had all the answers and as he aged and started losing his seeing his mind worked faster. He was the smartest man I ever met until Kenneth came a courting.

"I liked talking on the porch and so Kenneth and I stepped outside when Roberta brought him over to meet the family. You can't get to know a man until you get him away, somewhere quiet. We sat there on that front porch letting the sounds of the river bottoms fill us. Beautiful glittering fall night sky not too far from the river and the sounds of nighttime crickets and their rhythmic chirping.

"Kenneth and his mind were never much for sitting. He was just first meeting me, his soon to be mother n law and hadn't yet worked up the courage to ask for Roberta's hand. It would be coming sure as I was sitting. My bones had a sense to them, and Kenneth was talking to those types of yearnings that run through Davis women. Roberta was in love. Family kind of love. I had to see for myself what the boy was made of and what made him tick.

"That was when he blurted out that there had been a big explosion like never before. It's still moving, the velocity of a billion years ago keeping things in place but the farther away you go life is still trying to find balance, energy outside of the grounding forces of gravity, looking for a place to rest. Had to be a gigantic explosion. Long, long before us. Spaceships and time travel and on and on he would get too talking.

"He was like that. He would talk non-stop to and for the rest of my breathing days we would sit out there on the porch when he came visiting. Talking and yakking about those forces beyond the seeing. I loved my son-in-law."

##

Happy, engaged and effusive. National honor society and a smile. Great parents. A shining light in an all too dim world. And we didn't see it coming.

We have no cure for the disease that strikes young men and women. You lose friends, family, and yourself while the pills feel like death run over.

Schizophrenia. A split mind the Greeks said. The mind running at different speeds than the heart inside us. We give horse pills which slow the mind to a crawl. Going thru life with a 200-pound weight wrapped around your neck is not living less you think life in a dungeon with chains is living.

You can't see it. It's not like a broken arm or a leg covered with a cast. You hear them, you sense them. They come from the shadows. They grab you and take you to away. Other folks can't see or hear the voices and what isn't seen can't be real. Parents see the slow dying as the dreams they once had slowly die.

Old friends, coaches see the change. You don't laugh like yesterday. You don't talk like you once did. Your mind is floating like a knuckle ball and your heart is throwing high heat. 2 hours later your heart feels like a knuckle ball moves and your mind is seeing and throwing curveballs. A split mind, disconnected.

Schizophrenics are like fireworks on a beautiful summer night that have their moment and die. David was that shining light gone way to soon. Share your laughter David as you say hello to that other side of living. RIP.

##

It was a sad day. A real sad day when I heard my friend moved on. My heart dropped and I thought of her family and friends who meant everything to Big Nance. My deepest sympathy to Tom and family who were filled with the spirit of Nancy Cofield Neeser.

In life you meet few people like Big Nance. When you do you hold 'em. We shared cups of coffee, nearly 300 miles apart, and talked of the town and the people we loved.

She was a bit older and far more sophisticated than this broken-down author but somehow, some way the forces of modern technology brought us together. She had one of the biggest hearts I've come across as her words jumped off the page.

I remember sitting in Blooming Grounds, having a cup of coffee, and chatting with her about all that happened back in the day. We tapped on the keyboard the musings of the times. She was in class the day that JFK got shot, remembering the exact classroom and teacher, and she was there when her parents, Frank and Naomi, got the call in the fall of 1965 that their son, Nancy's brother Steve, had died in a plane crash outside of Fulton, Missouri.

She remembered Martin Luther King and Bobby Kennedy. Malcolm X, John Steinbeck and Edna Farber who all took their last breaths in that year she graduated. Somehow the fires in American cities that blazed in the 60's and the cops of Chicago didn't dampen the deeply American spirit that was Nancy.

If anything, the light, the torch she believed in burned brighter as the days passed right up to her dying days. She kept her smile, her spark, and her resolve as the America she grew up in exploded and unraveled. She never stopped fighting for the decency of our human spirit.

Peace, my dear friend and if we meet in a story or on the other side, I'll keep up the fight we so believed in.

Yesterday and Today

I like walking the streets of Winona town. I like looking at old houses and storefronts no longer the same, different names on the mailbox and I ask myself who is going to remember yesterday when we are gone.

A way of life, slower and deeper is leaving as this crazy life we have created has bitten our backside. Hurry, hurry, get this done so we can be somewhere else. And 'tomorrow is more of the same as yesterday' has done disappeared. Whitewashed and homogenized as we stood by rushing to be somewhere else.

The corner grocery stores are gone and the neighborhoods where everybody knew everybody have followed suit. Backyards where kids jumped fences and played ditch, where kids smoked their first cigarette and held hands, mostly gone. The landscape of our innocent years, gone.

Life goes faster. I remember Mr. Kulas teaching us computer language on punch cards at the old Jr. High just to get a computer to print out Hi or Welcome in those early days of computing. Those machines were just getting started and it seems like today those machines powered by computer chips and electricity and a world we could not have imagined have all trampled our ways. Back when things were thought out before jumping and it wasn't so hard to breathe.

The machines of industry and commerce churn fast. Electricity and computer chips, driving the machines that drive us faster. They see the world in different light those machines do, figuring and findings ways that our wise men might take years to calculate. I wonder if we are more than a digit in a file stored on another bigger computer.

The day will come when you can put your feet up and say tomorrow. I want to live in a town where space exists that has life moving slower. Where I don't have to worry about cars running over this slow-moving walking man. I want to be surrounded by people who have let grudges go and are searching for a better way. Neighborhoods brought that to us in our innocent years and I ask myself why not now?

The cars they move zip, zip, zip. Posted thirty and everybody going thirty-five or more. Us slow walkers can't barely get across some roads. You don't want me driving because I'm best puttering along five under that speed limit. So, stay home, out of our way I hear from the pick-up trucks as they buzz right by. A race, a race down Broadway, a four-lane road that cuts through the heart of the town which was and is a neighborhood. I pay my taxes as they yell step aside old man.

I sit in the Meditation garden on the Winona State Campus behind the Vivian Fusillo Theatre. I hear the sounds of students and feel the release of them being gone. I sit thinking about neighborhoods and the change that has gone through them. Where families once lived rental units fill the blocks and the neighborhood changes every fall.

We come from one car families and mom being home. Grandma and Grandpa not far away. Ride your bike and play cards, listen to a ball game or listen to grandpa in his garage tell you about that first car and the fun, the freedom it brought him.

How, oh how do we slowdown so the memories which helped form us can be part of our grandchild's life past the gravestone. A slower moving city affecting everyone who drives through. A place, to rest, relax, raise a family and listen to the sounds of the mighty Mississippi.

Too much energy in the relations amongst us. In the old days a cop might not hardly think about the guy in the car as you pulled him over for speeding. If I were a cop, a job I could never do, I would dread approaching a car on a traffic stop. Guns, guns everywhere just looking for a flash. I can't imagine the fear a black man must feel if something goes wrong in the light of history as the energies of living have separated us.

I pick myself up from the bench and start looking for what else is happening in Winona town as I walk the streets of yesterday in the light of today.

We were headed to Austin to see the grandkids. Both my grandfathers died early, and I never got to feel their wisdom. Josie calls me 'Crazy Grandpa', and I wear the badge with pride as I go about forgetting and going in the wrong direction.

Sometimes I stumble when I walk and other times I start talking about dinosaurs and birds. Birds, yellow ones, gold ones, red ones, a million colors under the sun and they all talk different.

We go get an ice cream cone. Brothers Vince and Wes are right behind, faces covered with ice cream and laughter.

We talk about the birds and trees, The rivers and the mighty glaciers which formed this land tens of thousands years ago. We talk of great dinosaurs which roamed the earth and big birds which that soared above us.

It was a beautiful day for being a Grandpa, I thought, as the kids peppered me with questions. No place I would rather be.

Tell him Happy Birthday.

I was sitting with the old man out at the cemetery. Just a couple days after Memorial Day. It was just before the downpour. Warm rain coming near straight down. Tale end of the Cristobal Hurricane as that moisture found a landing spot.

He told me he liked the rain. Made him feel fresh, clean. "Ma wasn't much for rain," he said.

I nodded my head having wondered where my rain loving came from. Love the smell and Science even has a name for it. Pluviophile. I like walking in the rain.

Dad told me early on that once you stop walking and start setting it gets harder and harder to get back up. He started talking about the Marines and I shook my head.

Some days sitting with Dad in the cemetery is like sitting in a rocking chair out on the porch of the Fremont store. "Grandpa," he said, "Used to have a place across the road. Tore down a couple years but inside that house was a big round room. In the middle of that room was a heating stove. Grandpa chewed and spat into an old gold spittoon. My Pa," he said, "Spat watermelon seeds further than any man I ever met. Those were the days before TV, so we had to entertain ourselves. It got quiet some days so we'd spit watermelon seeds, pick 'em up, wash them and do it again. Course there'd be some betting going on. Never had enough money to risk losing. Pa used to play a mean accordion, and I'm guessing that's where your brother got his musical leanings," he said.

He asked about the grandkids. Every single one of them. I told him about the great grandkids and that Lindsay was expecting come August. He got happy and his eyes kind of danced. Big grin, and then he felt the sadness of never being able to touch, hold and laugh.

The rain was falling pretty good. It's a nice sound hearing the rain fall on the tree.

"Tell Jeff how much I love him and wish him the happiest of birthdays."

I nodded.

He said, "Now get home before you catch a cold."

You notice the quiet as they go.

Happy Birthday Bro.

##

It was Father's Day so I headed out to the cemetery. I stopped at Hyvee, to pick up a flower and headed to his grave. Times change when you cross on over and so I had purchased a purple carnation. He was happy to see me and scratched his head when I handed him the purple flower.

"You've finally seen the light," he said.

I could feel my neck hair rising. Here he was, already giving me a hard time about being a Packer fan. Somethings don't change when you step on over.

We had our differences when living. Fathers and sons don't always get along. It's tough growing, learning and finding yourself on the road to manhood.

I told him, "Mom misses you. Even remembers you, though she does forget some nowadays. You've become more important to her now that you are gone. I think she misses the arguing."

Dad shrugged. "I'm much the same. People don't argue on this side. It's just a calm, quiet emotion running thru us. Oh, and football don't matter over here. Different priorities."

"Well, next year I'm bringing you a green and gold flower if it doesn't matter. A whole bouquet so the whole world knows you've become a Packer fan."

"Go ahead, tarnish my legacy. How are the kids?"

"Good. Headed to Ted's right after here. You need a lift?"

"No, Punk might swing by. The door is always open. We don't have to lock our doors over here you know. Did I ever tell you that getting you placed in a 72-Hour hold was perhaps the hardest thing I ever did in my life?"

I shook my head.

"I needed it. Freedom lost. It came back. I was one messed up person. But I got to meet Ernest."

"Ernest?"

"Hemingway. It was shocking. He died in 61 after all. First night I was in lock-up, he came a calling. We talked for a few hours and then he left. The nurses called it the Hemingway Suite, but I know they didn't see dead people. I wasn't about to tell them. It would have been St. Peter here I come."

"Life on the other side. Talk about blind. Never, ever thought

I would see life once more. What did Hemingway say?"

"Use small words and write like you are there."

He started fading and the hairs on the back of my neck relaxed. Fathers and sons on the road of life, listening to different tunes at different times. I heard the flag rippling from the flagpole, remembering old Marines never die. I started my car and headed to my son's.

##

The rain was lightly falling. It was the Trinona. I was volunteering as the kids swam, ran and biked. It was refreshing to see kids pushing themselves. It would be easy to stop, go back to the comfort of video games and TV. But here the kids were finding their own way, outside and in the elements.

The dead folk who came to watch showed me what Winona was. They were loud, encouraging these young boys and girls every step of the way. Thousands of people out watching kids trying to better themselves

A woman from the other side sat next to me and started talking. "Most of us didn't have a thing when we first started. We came to Winona poor. We came from the small towns, the poor desolate farms, eager for work. Winona was the best. So many things to do. That's why I loved this town and its people."

I had never met her, but she resembled an old friend who grew up on Fifth between the tracks and Jefferson. She told me her name was Sylvia.

"Most of us have no blood in the game. Our kids have moved to bigger cities. More money. I'm not sure happiness is found in the pot at the end of that rainbow," her husband, Ed, said.
"Families broken. Grandparents 100 miles away from their grandchildren. These are the kids of Winona, though not my own, who I choose to support. Caring about kids is who I was. A better tomorrow ran thru my whole life. It wasn't about me."

The rain cooled my face. I felt myself relaxing, letting go of the mess that is today. Eying yesterday and tomorrow coming together. Folks I hadn't seen in years, decades, and sometimes forever, showing up to provide support to the adults of tomorrow. You never saw so many happy people as the spirit that was Winona shone bright.

##

Fall wakes my bones, chills my heart, takes me back to old friends and long-ago places. I feel alive as the greens of summer lose their color.

It was 1977. It was a beautiful night. Black skies and brilliant lights. I could breathe in the clear air of St. Mary's College. It was 3 AM and I was drinking Jack and smoking cheap weed on the stoop of St. Marys Hall.

It was the early to middle stages of leaving reality and I carry that journey with me today. The road was bumpy, and I was driving fast on that road to expulsion. Living in the deep end not knowing where I was headed.

"I should have killed him," the white throat said as he sat down next to me. "I danced when he died. I felt free from the burden Bishop Heffron held over me. Brain Cancer they say. I say it was the devils seed sprouting."

He walked with a cane, small in stature, thin and his eyes burned bright like a true believer. His beard had turned white. Father Louis he said.

"We never liked each other. From the moment we met. Heffron thought he was God. I was a humble servant who walked the path of Jesus and refused to be bullied."

I poured another Jack and took a long drag off my smoke. Talking with the dead folk. One of the first in a long line of meeting dead folk. I wanted to run but I heard the whisper of my dad. Sons of Marines don't run. Face the music. Dad ever present.

"I plotted killing Heffron for a long time. I shot him on the second floor and fled to my room. Room 135, St. Marys Hall. If you listen, you can still hear the gun shots echoing off the marble halls, floors and walls. Echo's, of yesterday and that Monday morning in 1915.

"No regrets other than I only planned for three shots. Father, Son, Holy Ghost. Three shots. Dead. Heffron was all Father, and I was the Son with groundings in the Holy Spirit on the spiritual journey of a priest."

"Now like you Hanson, I wasn't quite right in the head. It was 1915 and I dreaded the gray days of winter I wouldn't leave my bed, my room for days on end in the dark days of winter. I was trapped and the wisdom of the time was to accept what the lord had given you. Carry on.

"My myths came from the French revolution of my forefathers. My family was not one of wealth. My great grandfather met St. John Baptiste De LaSalle and his followers of Christian brothers who raised this institution to its greatness. Heffron, with his fancy robes and displays of wealth, was not one of us.

"You should get rest Hanson. Your journey has just started, and you will need your strength. I died in 43 and I rest in the second cemetery in St. Peter. The home of the criminally insane. Come visit and I will tell the rest of my story."

##

I don't understand why older generations blame Millennials. We're leaving chaos and such a mess in this world for our kids to clean up, and then we have the audacity to blame those kids for the mess we're leaving them. That's insane. These days, the voices in my head talk to me in kind and gentle tones. They haven't always done that.

The shadows start dancing inside my thinking, and I'm not sure that what I'm seeing is made up or real. Senses I didn't realize I had have entered my being, and it feels like there are puppet masters pulling strings beyond what I can see.

I was only nineteen years old when the thousand voices started rumbling through me. I was nineteen and hearing the voices of the dead. That experience is not for the weak-souled. I was at a party, and I was absolutely filled with this very bright light, and it allowed me to see for the first time. It freed me.

I couldn't see the voices that were talking beyond my seeing. Those sounds of my disease, of what the doctors sometimes called schizophrenia, sometimes manic depression, came as voices from dead bodies. To fear what was beyond what I could see makes for a very long, hard disease. It was 30 years of listening to those many, many voices before I began to shape what they told me into stories and get them out through my fingertips.

The voices tell me their stories, and it fills my bones, shakes them. The glass walls of my thinking became broken, shattered, splinters of glass everywhere.

My dad and I never saw eye to eye. We were just opposites in about every way. When he died, it was like a release. We're still very different from each other, but now that he's dead, we talk just fine.

These dead people are more real than the people I know. They're more real because they talk with me and they let me ask them questions and they tell me details about their lives.

People who think they already know all they need to know to live in this life just baffle me. I think people who are good at something are often a little bit different. I have no problem with calling myself a little crazy because I am. I've accepted it. I think my mental illness allows me to question things more. It's just another way of looking at the world. It's like a new window opened, that I can look through and see new things, and I have a pretty big window to look through. Some people are trapped by the narratives of their past, but I'm able to step outside of that.

I've met some of the coolest people I've known in psychiatric units. There were many, many people there who were exceptionally smart.

Even when I was young, I heard whispers and sensed shadows and saw dead people. But there was nothing wrong with me; I just couldn't process everything that was happening. You don't "contract" a mental illness. It just shows up on your doorstep and demands to be dealt with. I have blind spots, like everyone does, but I feel fortunate to have the ability to look at things the way I do.

And now I view the voices of the dead as a gift. These people show up, and I listen to them. They have given me their stories of living in this town. Everywhere I go, I see ghosts. I can feel when a story is getting ready to come out because my joints and bones ache.

Today, as I edge closer to the grave, I give thanks to the dead and all their voices.

##

History has long talked to me. Part of my disease is seeing light through different prisms of time. It ain't so bad. Welcome.

Anyway, it was spring. I was restless. I've gotten better at getting out in the winter, but the bones just don't work as well. I imagine someday, they'll have chips inside us that lubricate our bones. Never fast, mostly plodding even at the best of times, and I've gotten worse. Science girl calls me a sloth.

Its spring and I'm feeling a bit frisky. The bite of winter wakes me up, jolts my senses. Part of my manhood complex. Runs deep in the ancient hinterlands of the family myth. It doesn't necessarily run fast.

I like benches to sit on. I can sit for hours, staring and talking to things seen and not. I hear yesterday, and the stories of the people and the buildings present and not. Dad liked benches too. It's in my genes.

I know it's a bit off the beaten path. Not a career choice I would recommend. Here, seated on the corner of Fourth and Center, I can say that now. Back then if I'd a told you I was hearing the voices you would have locked me up. The sound of a metal door closing leaves an imprint on this man who needed time.

It was my secret. Hush, hush was the word. I didn't tell my Psychiatrist, nor my priest, nor the bartender, that I heard the sounds. Life moves slower when you take those horse pills. Like a 200 pounds of ball and chain around your neck. Each step is harder.

It doesn't stop, those pills, the disconnect between your mind and body. It slows things down. Takes the reaction out of living. I needed that then. There is a break in that connect between your thoughts and feelings. Like seeing the world in two different speeds at the same time. And they dance. Schizo and Phrenia are a combination Greek word for split and mind.

Any way I've had my say. Might be time to move on to the next bench. Hunker down, brothers and sisters. Hunker down.

Made in the USA
Middletown, DE
23 November 2022